THE GHOSTLY GROUNDS:

DEATH

AND

BRUNCH

(A CANINE CASPER COZY MYSTERY—BOOK 2)

SOPHIE LOVE

Sophie Love

#1 bestselling author Sophie Love is author of THE INN AT SUNSET HARBOR romantic comedy series, which includes eight books; of THE ROMANCE CHRONICLES romantic comedy series, which includes 5 books; and of the new CANINE CASPER cozy mystery series, which included three books (and counting).

Sophie would love to hear from you, so please visit www.sophieloveauthor.com to email her, to join the mailing list, to receive free ebooks, to hear the latest news, and to stay in touch!

BOOKS BY SOPHIE LOVE

THE CANINE CASPER COZY MYSTERY SERIES
THE GHOSTLY GROUNDS: MURDER AND BREAKFAST (Book #1)
THE GHOSTLY GROUNDS: DEATH AND BRUNCH (Book #2)
THE GHOSTLY GROUNDS: MALICE AND LUNCH (Book #3)
THE GHOSTLY GROUNDS: VENGEANCE AND DINNER (Book #4)

THE INN AT SUNSET HARBOR
FOR NOW AND FOREVER (Book #1)
FOREVER AND FOR ALWAYS (Book #2)
FOREVER, WITH YOU (Book #3)
IF ONLY FOREVER (Book #4)
FOREVER AND A DAY (Book #5)
FOREVER, PLUS ONE (Book #6)
FOR YOU, FOREVER (Book #7)
CHRISTMAS FOREVER (Book #8)

THE ROMANCE CHRONICLES
LOVE LIKE THIS (Book #1)
LOVE LIKE THAT (Book #2)
LOVE LIKE OURS (Book #3)
LOVE LIKE THEIRS (Book #4)
LOVE LIKE YOURS (Book #5)

CHAPTER ONE

The sounds of hammering and drilling from outside should have sounded like progress to Marie. Instead, it sounded more like the cartoon sound effect of a cash register constantly dinging, the drawer opening for more and more of her money. With each nail Benjamin, her handyman, drove in, there went more money. With each rattling of the chain for the porch swing, more money. If Marie listened very hard, she thought she could hear her checking account crying digital tears.

If she had more than one guest currently staying in June Manor, the noises might not bother her as badly. It even made her wonder why she was trying to improve upon the place. If no one was coming, why bother updating it?

She knew the answer. While the bed-and-breakfast had seen its share of controversy and negative publicity lately, her hope was that it would all blow over soon enough. After all...not everyone had heard the news. Not everyone knew that she had gone so far as to claim her bed-and-breakfast was haunted only to have it essentially proven false. The news had more or less been confined to some very specific niches of the internet—and, of course, the small local population of Port Bliss. Surely things would get back to normal...right?

That was the hope. But it was a fleeting hope, especially considering her plans for the night. She was nervous about them, maybe even a little scared. But there was twenty thousand dollars waiting for her at the end of it. And with that sort of cushion in the June Manor checking account, maybe the sounds Benjamin was making out on the porch wouldn't be so intimidating.

Marie was sitting at the dining room table, close enough so that she could hear Benjamin's progress and have some idea what was taking place, but far enough away to not be too traumatized over it all. She glanced at her cell phone every few moments, anticipating the phone call that would get what promised to be a very strange night started.

As she waited, she heard her front door open. Very few people ever entered June Manor without knocking first, so she knew it was Posey. Sure enough, her kind and very talented cook came walking into the dining room. She carried no bags, indicating that whatever dinner she cooked tonight for the single guest would come from ingredients she already had stashed away in the fridge.

"Benjamin almost has the swing up," Posey said. "It's going to look very nice." She hesitated before entering the kitchen and gave Marie a curious glance. "Something wrong?"

"Oh, there's plenty wrong. But at this very moment, I'm simply wondering if I'm about to make a big mistake."

"Oh, that's right! I almost forgot. It's like a date, right? With you and Brendan?"

Hearing his name sent a few different emotions through her. After all, Brendan Peck was the man who had caught the footage that made her believe the house was haunted. And then he had disproven it to save both himself and Marie from being eyed in a murder investigation. Such a strange turn of events was bound to give her mixed feelings about a person. But it also didn't help that Brendan seemed to be very genuine. And that she was doing all she could to fight off a minor crush she had on him.

"Um, absolutely not," Marie said. "Sitting in a house and hoping my dog can scare a ghost out of a house is not a date."

"But you'll be along with him, right?" Posey said with a teasing smile. "Like all night?"

"You're awful, Posey. But…you're also an angel. You're certain you're okay running the place tonight?"

"Honey, there's one person. And I have Benjamin's number saved into my phone. Yes, I think I can handle it. I do wish you were leaving Boo with me, though. I sort of like that mutt."

Summoned by his name, Boo came walking into the room. He looked up at Posey expectantly and wagged his tail when she scratched him between the ears. "You gonna go bust that mean old ghost tonight, boy?"

His tail wagged even faster at Posey's high-pitched voice. He followed her into the kitchen, perhaps hoping she might drop a crumb or two as she set about prepping for dinner. This left Marie alone again, sitting at the dining room table and trying to convince herself that she wasn't about to make a huge mistake. How was she supposed to distance herself from the supernatural community if she was so willingly walking right back into it?

When her phone rang, she almost let out a little shout of fear.

Oh yeah, she thought. *Terrified of a phone. You're going to do just great tonight. Thank goodness Brendan Peck is also going to be there.*

Posey would have rather enjoyed the smile that came to Marie's face when she saw Brendan's name on her phone's caller display. Even though she *knew* it would be him, seeing the confirmation made her feel safer somehow. It was weird…and she did not like the way it made her feel.

"Hey there," she said. "Long time no see…or talk."

"Not too long," Brendan said. "Four days, right?"

"I'm not counting." But she was. And yes, he was right; it had been four days.

"Well, you better," he said. "Look, Marie, I hate to do this to you but I can't be there tonight."

The first thing Marie felt was terror. But then there was a fleeting sadness from realizing she would not see Brendan. The terror eventually won out, though. The proprietor of the bed-and-breakfast had made it quite clear that tonight would be the only night in a very long time she could open the house up in such a way. So it was basically now or never. And while Marie would have preferred to choose *never*, she could not turn down the money.

"And you're sure she can't reschedule?" she asked.

"No. It's got to be tonight."

She felt nerves starting to boil up in her stomach. There was fear, too, but it was an unrealized fear. It was a fear that seemed to nudge at her common sense and say: *Yeah, but we're not really going to do this, are we?*

"What? Wait…hold on. You were the one that talked me into doing this. And now you're not going to be there?"

"I know, I know. But there's this convention in Rhode Island. One of the featured guests got sick and can't make it. I got the call this morning, asking if I could step in tonight as a back-up. I know it might seem selfish, but it could be a huge step in salvaging my career."

The explanation really drove it home and she could feel her fear taking control of everything, worming its way through her like a weed. She wasn't sure she'd ever felt genuine fear like this before. The irony of it was that if she hadn't seen some of the things Brendan had brought into her life, she might not be so scared. And even though she wasn't a committed believer in his ghostly encounters and theories just yet, she'd been a part of enough to know what she *could* be walking into…alone.

And even further in the back of her mind was that she'd get over there (alone!) and it would turn out that Boo's little performance in June Manor had been a fluke. And the last thing Marie needed attached to her already strained reputation in Port Bliss was the term *fraud.*

"And you expect me to just go over there alone?"

"Marie, you'll be okay. Boo will be with you."

"Yes. I will be in the company of a dog."

"A dog with some rather special abilities, I might add." Brendan sighed. Something in it seemed far more remorseful than anything he had said to that point. "I really am very sorry, Marie. Look…if you don't want to do it, I'll call Mrs. Grace and let her know."

In the back of her mind, Marie was already saying the same thing over and over again, like a chant or mantra: *you need the money.* And the amount of money coming her way if she went to this other bed-and-breakfast and Boo was able to do his thing was very generous.

"What if I get over there and get possessed by a demon or something?" Marie asked. She meant it as a joke, but she'd seen that movie—the little girl floating above her bed and puking pea soup or something all over the priest. It was a cruel irony; her usual defense mechanism against all things was actually making her even more terrified.

"Don't joke about that, Marie. Look, if you do get over there and things seem to get a little out of control, there are a few things you can do. First…make sure you take a Bible. You know any scripture?"

"Um…not really."

"Doesn't matter. Find a passage where Christ is demanding demons to flee and—"

"Wait, you're serious?"

"I am. And if the Bible thing seems weird to you, there's always salt. Even modern-day ghost hunters believe that standing in a ring of salt will keep you safe from violent spirits. Something about earth energy—"

"Brendan! Is this supposed to make me feel better?"

"Look, Marie. I hope you know I wouldn't send you on your own if I thought it was dangerous."

"Yeah, I know."

"See you soon?"

She couldn't waste the opportunity to get in the last jab. "I guess that would be up to you."

She hung up the phone, smiling. Boo had ventured back into the room, looking up at her with a knowing glare. The dog did creep her out on occasion. For instance, right now it looked as if he knew that she was bothered—that he had heard every single word of the conversation she'd just had—on both sides of the phone.

"What do you say, Boo? You ready?"

In response, he wagged his tail, got up, and started for the front door.

Marie looked out her front window where Benjamin was currently directing a local subcontractor up an old birch tree. The limbs were too close to the house and needed to be pruned back. She watched them, but distantly. She thought about what tonight might bring and how it might affect her reputation if she just called it off. She was in way over her head even if it *was* Boo that was doing all of the work. Yeah, she needed the money, but was it worth the trouble and the fear? Was it worth—

Her thoughts were broken by the sound of a cracking branch and then a strange metallic tearing sound. She looked to the right and saw that the first branch to come off of the birch tree had landed directly on the left edge of the porch—and had torn down half of the gutter.

She sighed, already estimating the cost. And just like that, she knew that there was no way she could *not* go along with her original plans tonight.

CHAPTER TWO

Marie looked out the windshield, taking in the sight of the old bed-and-breakfast. She cocked her head, as if trying to see it better from a different angle, but it all remained the same. She frowned; it made no sense to her.

"This is the place?" Marie asked, looking at Boo. "This is the bed-and-breakfast?"

Boo was sitting in the back seat, regarding the place as if he were a potential guest.

The house itself had a grandiose sort of feel to it, but it was somewhat depleted by the gloomy-looking exterior. It simpler terms, it looked borderline creepy and decrepit. It made June Manor look like some bright and shiny palace from a Pixar movie.

"Well, Boo, I suppose we don't run the gamut on creepy and potentially haunted bed-and-breakfasts anymore." She chuckled at her own joke but realized afterward that it wasn't funny.

Boo let out a low chuffing noise. He seemed to share Marie's sentiments.

"What if it doesn't work?" Marie asked.

Boo whined and pawed innocently at the door. It was as if he knew they were supposed to be here…and that he had work to do.

"Okay, we'll go. Just…don't be mad at me, okay? I have to take the credit for this to work. You understand that, right?"

Boo only continued to paw at the door.

Marie looked back at the house. While June Manor had a gothic feel to it, this house took it to a whole different level. It looked like a miniaturized castle of sorts, airlifted straight out of Transylvania and plopped down in the tiny town of Bloom, Maine. The cutest and most traditional detail to the entire place was the hand-carved sign hanging over the wide front porch steps that read BLOOM GARDENS AND REST. In Marie's estimation, it was the one solitary thing that made the exterior look welcoming. Sure, the place had been well-maintained, but it screamed *house of horrors* rather than *come have a restful night's sleep inside me.*

In other words, she was getting her first taste of what so many others apparently thought of June Manor.

"Twenty thousand dollars," Marie said to herself. "Just remember that."

As she and Boo got out of the car and crossed the small yard to the front porch, Marie took a moment to reassess how she had ended up here. She certainly couldn't assume that her three weeks of bed-and-breakfast ownership gave her any right to go into Bloom Gardens and Rest and tell the owner what needed to be done—that was for sure. After all, she was only entertaining this woman's request for the money so she could keep her own B&B afloat—a B&B that had already endured its share of supernatural activity and controversy.

As they neared the porch, it occurred to Marie that if this bed-and-breakfast was legitimately haunted, she was willingly stepping inside. While she was somewhat fine with admitting that the paranormal had something of a foothold in her own B&B, it was an entirely different matter to willingly walk into a place that was, by the owner's own words, "being disrupted numerous times on a nightly basis."

When she stepped up onto the porch, Marie froze for a moment. Was that her imagination, or had the world gone a bit colder?

Boo trotted up the rest of the stairs and waited at the door. Marie followed him and knocked. It made a hollow sound that Marie was sure her already-spooked mind was making out to be much more horrifying than it actually was.

The woman who answered the door stood in direct opposition of the appearance of the house. She looked to be fifty or so, and was dressed in a light yellow summer dress. Her hair was blonde, though she had elected not to go to great lengths to hide the smattering of gray along the roots.

The woman eyed Marie for a moment and took a while to make a smile. Apparently, she was just as weirded out about the situation as Marie was.

"You're Marie Fortune, I assume?" the woman asked.

"Yes ma'am."

"Good to meet you, Marie. My name is Anna Grace, owner of Bloom Gardens and Rest." She then looked down, seeing Boo for the first time. "Oh my, and who is this?"

7

Boo knew praise when he heard it and went directly to the feet of his new friend. Mrs. Grace scratched him under the chin and rubbed his head.

"This is Boo. And if it's okay with you, I'd really appreciate it if he could come in with me. He's my sidekick."

"Oh dear," Mrs. Grace said. "I do love dogs, and this one seems like a sweetheart, but I have never allowed dogs in my house."

Marie felt her heart seize up in her chest. Oh, that would be perfect—to come all the way out here only to have her secret weapon not allowed in the house. It wouldn't take very long for her to be found out as a fraud if Boo wasn't able to come in with her. A small flare of panic sparked within her, but she figured she could at least try to convince Mrs. Grace.

"Oh, I see. Well, he is sort of an integral part of the process. It's...well, it's quite hard to explain." But what she was really thinking was that if Boo was not allowed to come in, the entire situation would crumble. She'd be known as a huge fraud by this time tomorrow.

"I assume he's housebroken?" Mrs. Grace asked.

"He is. And he barely sheds at all. If you like, I can even vacuum the house for you before I leave."

Mrs. Grace seemed irritated as she mulled it over. She looked down at Boo and the dog seemed to know he was the topic of discussion. He panted a bit and sniffed at Mrs. Grace's feet.

"I'll allow it," Mrs. Grace said. "Just please keep a careful eye on him."

The relief Marie felt was instant, but she tried to play it cool by giving a simple yet polite: "Thanks."

Mrs. Grace nodded and looked outside, where the afternoon was dwindling away into dusk. While she had agreed on meeting at this time with Brendan several days ago, she seemed to be regretting it. "Come on in, both of you, and I'll give you the tour."

Mrs. Grace led her inside. And as Marie walked in through the front door, she once again felt the world go just a touch colder. She looked down at Boo to see if he was behaving out of the ordinary, but he seemed completely unbothered. If anything, he looked excited about exploring a new house.

"I can't be certain," Mrs. Grace said, leading them into the quaint foyer, "but I believe there are two of them. One seems to be friendly, and the other quite mean."

"Two of *them*?"

"Ghosts, dear."

So it was going to be like that, Marie thought. No beating around the bush, no dancing around the spectral elephant in the room. There was something refreshing about it, but also sort of disarming. *Brendan must have loved this lady,* Marie thought.

Marie was listening intently, but she was also taking the time to take the place in. She supposed it had more in common with June Manor than she'd originally thought. Once she got inside, it looked a bit more regal—albeit still spooky. Bloom Gardens and Rest was a two-story building, but it felt as confined as a one-story. It was a peculiar feeling. The ceiling in the foyer was at least twenty feet tall, dipping only the slightest bit as the house gave way to its other rooms. The foyer floor was made of something that resembled subway tile, making a smooth transition into the hallway that appeared to lead off into several bedrooms. Much like June Manor, the stairway to the second level was one of the first things to see as she walked through the front door.

"Did Brendan tell you much about the house?" Mrs. Grace asked.

"Not much," she said. "I think he was saving that for you."

Mrs. Grace led them into a small living area occupied by beautiful plush furniture. Marie took a seat on a small loveseat while Mrs. Grace settled into a stately-looking recliner. Boo sat at Marie's feet.

"It's been going on for years," Mrs. Grace said. "At first, it was small things. The salt and pepper shakers would move from the kitchen counter to the powder room sink. The table umbrellas out on the back porch would be closed just as soon as I opened them. My favorite, though, was on a few occasions when I'd have Frank Sinatra playing on my Bluetooth speaker, and there would be this hiss of static and then the Beatles would be playing. And it was *always* 'Strawberry Fields.' Little things like that."

"But it got worse?" Marie asked.

"Yes. About six or seven months ago, I got the sense that there was another one. That all these playful little things were from one ghost. And honestly, I don't know that it ever bothered my guests. I had a few people talk about how they thought they saw something out of the corner of their eye, or how their personal items would go missing only to return to their bedside table right before check-out. But then this other…this other *presence* showed up and it all changed.

"As an example, guests would come to me in the morning swearing that there was this imposing figure standing by the foot of their bed. I even had one couple from Virginia swear that something actually lifted the bed a little bit. Those poor folks checked out of here at two in the morning. The husband looked as white as snow."

"Have you *seen* either of the figures?" Marie asked.

"I think I've seen the mean one. I know when it's in the room with me because it gets so damned *cold*. And when I tell it to get out, it does….but it's reluctant. And when it leaves, there have been a few times where I almost see something moving—like a blurred shadow."

"Is there a dark history to the house?" Marie asked.

"Yes, though I knew none of it until after I purchased it eight years ago. There are police reports that give details of a woman who killed her husband in self-defense. And there are also many rumors around here that claim the man that built the house—the original owner, I suppose—hung himself on the front porch during a thunderstorm."

Marie shuddered and did her best to hide it. She wanted to leave very badly but, at the same time, couldn't seem to pull herself out of the seat.

"There's one other thing, too," Mrs. Grace added. "My mother used to swear the house she was raised in had a ghost or two in it. She passed away many years ago…and the house was eventually demolished by some big builder. When Mr. Peck was here looking the place over, he told me that such a thing is not unheard of—that there are stories of ghosts sticking with certain families even after they've moved into another house. That could be the case here."

"I see," Marie said. But she didn't. She just felt the need to say something so the house wouldn't fall into silence.

"Anyway," Mrs. Grace said, "if you need me, I'll be going to my other house. I live here most of the time, but have been spending more and more time at my little cottage outside of town ever since this second ghost has showed up."

"You won't be here?" Marie asked. It felt like the bottom had fallen right out of her stomach.

"No, dear. I don't think anything here can harm me, but I'd still rather not be around if you tend to aggravate my unwanted guests. I'm so sorry…did Brendan not tell you I would not be staying?"

"No, he failed to mention that part." She tried to hide her irritation, as she had no quarrel at all with Mrs. Grace. But Brendan was sure going to get a few choice words if she ever saw him again.

"Well, I'm terribly sorry, but I feel that it might be very strange if I stayed here. I've already made plans and I'd rather not change them."

"Of course not," Marie said. The terror blooming in her heart was almost paralyzing. Even getting those three words out was difficult and there was a childlike waver to her voice that she hoped Mrs. Grace did not hear.

"Ms. Fortune, I do wish you the best of luck," Mrs. Grace said, already walking toward the door. "If you should need anything at all, my number is on the refrigerator. And help yourself to anything in the fridge, by the way."

"Thanks. You know, I wonder if—"

"Oh, I'm sure you'll do fine. Thank you so much for doing this! I'll see you in the morning." She opened the door and then, as an afterthought, added: "Maybe be careful about the first bedroom on the second floor. That room in particular is usually pretty...*active*."

"What do you m—"

Mrs. Grace left so quickly that Marie felt the gust of air left behind by the door as she closed it. When the door shut behind her, Marie felt that it was a concrete slab being pushed in front of a tomb.

"All right," Marie said, looking at Boo. "Get to work, boy. Let's get this over with and get out of here."

Boo looked at her quizzically but then turned and started walking through the house as if he had understood her perfectly. Marie paid very close attention to every nook, cranny, and corner, but was also mentally drafting up a nasty text message that she would soon be sending to Brendan Peck.

Boo, meanwhile, walked through the house as if he owned the place, taking a moment here and there to sniff things of interest. Marie followed him around for a while but when it was clear that he was doing his own thing, Marie summoned up as much courage as she could find and started taking a self-guided tour of the house.

There were four bedrooms downstairs, all of which were essentially the same: queen-sized beds with soft-colored linens, each bed sitting on a large decorative rug that covered about half of the rooms' well-kept hardwood floors. They also visited Mrs. Grace's bedroom, and then what looked like a den—a communal room of sorts where Marie could picture guests drinking coffee or tea, reading books, and chatting.

She then went upstairs where there were two more bedrooms identical to the ones downstairs. Boo was trailing behind her now and as he rushed ahead, Marie remembered Mrs. Grace's last warning—that the first bedroom upstairs was particularly active. She only glanced into the room. But even in that brief encounter, she could absolutely feel something strange about the room. For just a moment, it felt like she was sticking her head into an old chasm that had gone centuries without human contact.

But as soon as she stepped out of the room, it was gone. She shook the feeling off, but noted that Boo had walked in for a moment and seemed to be interested in something. Whatever it was only held his attention for a moment before he turned around and headed back out into the hallway.

At the end of the hallway was a larger room that served as a game room. There was a pool table and a dartboard, but they were both covered. A small bookcase also held a variety of board games. From the look of the room alone, Marie got the feeling that the room was rarely used.

The tour ended back downstairs in the kitchen, and then out on the large back porch. The back porch seemed to be the only modernized thing about the house; the fresh lumber was a telltale sign that it had recently been remodeled or repaired. The porch looked out over a long field that actually looked quite stunning as the sun set—the gardens from the name of the bed-and-breakfast. It had nothing on the beach view from the back porch of June Manor, but it had its own sort of quiet charm.

After the back porch, Marie returned to the little living room. As she reclaimed the seat she'd occupied before, she tried to make herself relax. Maybe this was all a big hoax of some kind. Maybe Mrs. Grace had heard about what had happened with June Manor and was playing an elaborate prank on her.

But as the afternoon lugged in the dusk and the yard outside grew darker, she somehow sensed that those were all just hopes and wishful thinking. Even Boo seemed to get a little unnerved as night approached.

"It's okay, Boo," she said. "And I'm so sorry I put you in this situ—"

She was interrupted by a soft clunking noise that came from the kitchen. Both Marie and Boo swiftly turned their heads. Marie's shoulders went tense and Boo's tail went rigid. Marie felt herself getting to her feet and knew what she was about to do. She tried to tell herself not to, but before she knew it, she was on her feet and running for the door.

CHAPTER THREE

She dashed through the foyer and back out onto the porch, leaping down the stairs. She stopped, panting for breath, realizing that she had not been that scared in a very long time. It was embarrassing but also refreshing in a way she almost appreciated. She then looked all around, at the night falling along the edges of a porch where, sometime in the past, a man may or may not have hung himself.

Slowly, and with much embarrassment, Marie walked back toward the house. Fear still paraded in her heart, but she was aware of what could be at stake here. Twenty grand. A reputation…of sorts. In other words, too much. And for the first time this evening, she was actually *glad* that neither Mrs. Grace nor Brendan were there.

When she went back into the living room, Boo was there to greet her. He stayed by her side as she walked through the living room and into the kitchen. She didn't have to scan the room for very long to see what had caused the noise. There was a crystal saltshaker in the middle of the kitchen floor. It had most definitely *not* been there when she and Boo had made their initial circuit of the house. The little shaker had not broken, but the lid had popped off. Salt had spilled out onto the floor. Boo slowly walked over to the salt, sniffed it, and then turned his head in disgust.

"Think it might have just fallen?" Marie asked.

This was more wishful thinking, as the pepper shaker that was its twin was on the side of the stove, at least four feet away.

Boo sniffed at the spilled salt again. He then looked up to his master and let out a little whine.

Marie shuddered and thought: *My sentiments exactly, boy.*

***

Night settled in around Bloom Gardens and Rest like a dark sheet over a mattress, though there was nothing as comforting about it. Marie wasn't exactly sure what she should be doing, as this was really Boo's

14

show. She was having a hard enough time convincing herself to stay in the house after having heard the stories from Mrs. Grace.

And the little scene with the saltshaker hadn't helped, either.

Oh my God, what am I even doing here?

She saw a pie graph in her head that she tried to ignore, but it provided the answer. Ninety-eight percent of the pie chart was covered in green, pointing at the hefty payday. The other two percent was colored yellow and was labeled: *To impress Brendan.*

Thinking of him, Marie took out her phone while standing in the kitchen and typed a much briefer text than she had planned. It read: **So…Mrs. Grace isn't staying here. You knew this????**

She figured he was busy with the convention and would not answer for a while, but she sent it anyway.

Or, rather, she tried to. She got the little dots, letting her know it was *trying* to send. But the message stayed there. She had a good signal and—

But as she watched, the signal was depleted from almost full to absolutely dead. The same thing happened to her battery indicator. As she held the phone, she watched the battery not just trickle away, but go from forty-five percent battery life to in the red within five seconds. And then the phone died altogether.

"What the hell?"

She'd never had a single problem with her phone. It was less than a year old and had always worked perfectly. It made her mind instantly jump to the next (not so) logical conclusion: it was the house. Somehow, the house or the supposed forces in it were manipulating her phone.

She left the kitchen, wondering if there was some sort of "dead spot" in the room. But the phone remained just as dead in the living room, the den, and the hallway.

As she slowly walked around the house with Boo by her side, she could instantly feel a shift to the place; it had become more noticeable after her phone went dead. She wasn't necessarily getting those little cold chills anymore, but was instead experiencing a sluggishness. As she made her way down the hallways, checking each of the bedrooms, she almost started to feel as if the floor was made of hot rubber, making it harder for her to walk.

She kept thinking of what Brendan had told her—that he would not willingly send her into a situation where he thought there was a chance she might be hurt. She believed him, but also knew that their tolerances for frightening things were quite different.

She made two laps of the house, not sure what she was looking for. She was scared out of her mind with every step she took, but the part of her that remained an astute skeptic was determined to figure out what seemed so *off* about this house. During the time she spent walking around the house, it occurred to Marie that she could very well be wasting her time. After all…*she* did not have the supernatural powers here. It was Boo. And for all she knew, the act he'd let loose upon the forces at June Manor could have been a fluke. So, realizing just how useless she was in this scenario, Marie went back to the living room. She figured it might be best not to watch TV; she didn't want to disrupt whatever ghosts or other forces were in the house. But at the same time, she couldn't quite handle the silence of the house, either.

In the end, she opted to turn the TV on and keep the volume low. She noticed right away that Boo seemed restless. He would sit with her for a while and then get down to take a lap around the house. He did this for an hour, as Marie started watching another episode of *The Good Place*. It was one of her favorite shows but because she was scared and uncertain, she wasn't finding it very comforting or funny.

It was already inching up to midnight and because she doubted she would be able to sleep, she figured she needed to try to keep her mind as focused as possible. With no phone and the drone of the TV not the best of mental exercises, she thought she might see what sort of books Mrs. Grace had lying around. She nearly got up to do this when she noticed that Boo was coming back into the room from one of his solo ventures.

He walked in a circle a few times and then settled at her feet. Apparently, he was done for the night and ready to sleep. *Good idea.* Marie felt her eyes drifting, drifting…and then she was out.

She jerked awake sometime later, having heard a noise from elsewhere in the house. She was shocked to find that she had drifted off—and even more shocked to find that the clock on the side table now read 3:07 AM.

She sat up, rubbing at her eyes and looking to the left, where she thought the sound had come from. As she looked out toward the hallway, she heard it again. She was right in that it was coming from that direction, but it also appeared to be coming from upstairs.

Boo walked toward the hallway and then looked back to her, as if to say: *Okay, lady, let's do this.*

Marie got up and silently thanked the dog for going first. She turned the lights on for the stairway and walked up behind Boo. As she saw the darkened upstairs hallway approaching, she was overcome with an old childhood fear of the dark. There was no telling what horrors waited up there, slobbering beasts ready to tear her apart, ghouls and goblins from under the earth, or—

Or nothing. She turned the light on and found an empty upstairs hallway. However, she did still hear the noise. It was a shifting sort of noise, like someone moving or sitting down on something soft.

It was coming from the first bedroom along the hallway, the one closest to her and Boo. The door was open and for the briefest of moments, Marie thought she could see *something* inside. The noise had been the creaking of bed springs and the ruffling of sheets—almost as if someone had been jumping on the bed. As she stood in the doorway, the wrinkled sheets, which had been perfectly straight when she'd come into the room the first time, made it quite clear that something had indeed been jumping on the bed.

"I guess that's the friendly one," Marie said.

Boo squeezed into the room between Marie's legs and the doorframe. He looked around curiously, cocked his head, and started wagging his tail.

At that same moment, there was a soft sound from elsewhere in the house—the kitchen, it seemed. Two sounds, then three, close behind one another. It was an easy enough sound to identify; in fact, Marie had heard the exact same sound in June Manor on her first full day there. It was footsteps…a sound that was a bit menacing, as the only person in the house right now was currently standing in the upstairs hallway.

"And I suppose that would be the other one," Marie said.

But then, as she was sure the footsteps had come from downstairs, they suddenly seemed to be in the hallway—just a few feet ahead of them. The hallway had grown cold and Marie was overcome with the sensation that they were definitely not alone.

Boo stood at her side, as solid and as rigid as a statue. His entire black body went rigid, his nose pointed outward as if he were some sort of well-trained hunting dog. His tail was slightly drooped between his legs, just as rigid as the rest of his body. A low growl started to come out of his throat, growing in volume with the passing of each second.

17

He was facing the hallway, sniffing and slowly cocking his head back and forth.

Boo stood like that for about ten seconds before he took a few tentative steps further into the hallway. He glanced forward and then, as if someone had slapped him on the backside to go after something, he turned and leaped into the bedroom. His growl became something more menacing as he moved. Marie had never heard him make such a sound, and it chilled her.

Boo's claws clicked furiously against the hardwood floor as he moved farther into the bedroom. As he went, Marie tried to tell herself that the cold gust of wind that swept across her body was only her imagination—but she knew it was not true.

Boo started to bark. There was no playfulness or joy in the barks. They were purely threatening, sounds of warning and danger. Marie stepped toward the doorway but paused, making sure to keep her distance and not interfere with whatever Boo was up to. While she did not like the idea of chasing after a dog that seemed to be on the hunt of a mean ghost, she also did not like the idea of missing out on the spooky excitement.

Boo's barks were now more like a series of violent yelps. Marie thought it might be the canine equivalent of cursing someone out. He was currently standing very close to the rear wall. He was barking loudly into the corner, as if he had cornered some unfortunate prey. Of course, there was no one or nothing in that corner—just empty space.

Boo repositioned himself, this time facing the bed, and continued barking and yelping. Marie strained her eyes, trying to see what he might be barking at, but it did no good. For the slightest of moments, Marie thought she could see the sheets on the bed move, as if someone had slid across the bed. But it could have also been a trick of the eyes, deceived by Boo's sudden and frantic motions.

At about that same time, Marie felt something cold pressing into her chest. It was startling, like being dropped into a frigid pool, but it was gone just as soon as it came. She took a single stumbling step backward and let out a gasp. Her breath was frozen in her lungs, but she was finally able to let it out when Boo went racing by her, back into the hall and down the stairs.

Marie followed him and by the time she reached the bottom of the stairs, Boo had stopped barking. He stared down the downstairs hall, back toward the living room. Slowly, his rigid posture relaxed. A small, thin whine came out of his throat, not one of sadness or pain, but something more like confusion.

Boo made a few steps toward the front of the house and then finally relaxed completely. He whined a bit, came trotting back to Marie, and rubbed against her leg. She leaned down to pet him, staring down the hallway.

"That's a good boy, Boo. You okay, bud?"

He wagged his tail to indicate that yes, he was okay. They walked down the hallway together, passed slowly through the kitchen, and then into the living room. Marie then walked back to the stairway and looked up.

"You feel that, boy?" she asked.

Boo sat down, also looking up the stairs. He was almost back to his normal self. Apparently, he did feel it.

Though, honestly, it wasn't necessarily feeling *something*...it was feeling *nothing*. She realized that the thick feeling she'd felt within the house—the oppressiveness that seemed to have made it harder to walk than usual—was no longer in the air.

"I think you did it," Marie told Boo. "I think they're gone."

She did indeed feel that this was the case. But at the same time, something within her could still not rest easy. Her mind raced with trying to make sense of what she had just witnessed. It wasn't just convincing her mind it had really happened; it was the sort of thing that could potentially skew a life view—a belief that there are things outside of the natural world that humans cannot see or control.

When her phone dinged twice in her pocket, she let out a little shout of surprise. She took it out at once and saw that Brendan had texted her twice while her phone had been dead. One text had come through at 10:30, the other at 12:12. Both were simple and to the point, simply checking on her.

Yo, you still alive? the first one read.

The second one read: **Won't lie. Starting to get a little scared for you. That dog of yours better keep you safe.**

She decided not to return the texts, as it was nearly 3:30 in the morning. But she looked at her phone, now working as if nothing had happened to it before, and then she slowly glanced around the house.

She'd seen Boo's little trick. And now her phone was working mere moments later.

The house felt different—*lighter* somehow. And as she let this sensation wash over her, she watched as Boo went into the living room, curled up on the rug, and fell into a well-deserved sleep.

CHAPTER FOUR

When Marie arrived back at June Manor shortly after nine the following morning, the guests she had left in Posey's care were coming down the stairs to check out. She was delighted to see that they looked well rested and happy. It took quite a bit of transition to slip back into the role of bed-and-breakfast owner after having spent a mostly sleepless night that involved watching her dog expel two ghosts from a house, but she did her best.

As for her dog, he immediately found his favorite spot on the sitting room floor and sprawled out comfortably. He looked very tired and also glad to be back home.

Posey was already angling herself into the little check-in desk inside the foyer to check the guests out. It was an older married couple who had spent most of the previous day out on the beach, just wanting some time away from the city.

"How was everything?" Marie asked as she took the room key from them.

"Oh, it's a lovely place," the wife said. "And the view of the beach at sunset from the back porch—it was the stuff of seasonal calendars."

"And I like the fact that the place isn't all modernized and trying to copy the cover of every interior design magazine," the husband said. "I felt like it's the sort of place that might have secret passages at every corner. Walking into the sitting room, I felt, for a moment, like I was in Hogwarts or something."

It was exactly the sort of thing she needed to hear. She wasn't sure if it was appropriate to find such pleasure in compliments but she thought it might be okay, given just how badly June Manor was struggling.

"I'm so glad to hear that," Marie said. "Please let your friends and family know about us!"

"We certainly will," the husband said on their way out. "And we'll be sure to leave a stellar review online."

The encouragement of her recently departed guests was almost enough to make her momentarily forget about the oddity she had witnessed last night. It also stirred up hope for the future. A few pleased guests scattered around the state or online could make all the difference.

And while hope was obviously good, it wasn't quite enough to have to accept the fact that her skeptical nature was starting to falter because of things she had witnessed. No, now she had to also accept the fact that her dog was apparently some sort of four-legged ghostbuster. Part of her couldn't help but wonder if his so-called talent was such a miraculous thing after all. Hadn't she read somewhere that animals—dogs in particular—had a sixth sense about certain things? There were dogs and wolves that could sense when earthquakes were coming. There were therapy cats that could not only detect when people were sick, but when they were approaching their final breathing moments.

As Marie headed back inside to get a better grasp on her day, she found Posey standing in the sitting room, waiting for her. "And how was *your* night?" she asked.

"It was …weird. But that's not even the right word. I don't even know how to explain it. And I really don't want to talk about it. Honestly, I just want to grab some breakfast. Maybe a nap if I can manage it. I didn't really sleep all that well."

"Well, the breakfast thing I can provide," Posey said. "As a matter of fact, if you'll follow me into the dining room…"

She did not finish her sentence. Instead, she started walking in the direction of the kitchen and dining room. Marie followed, taking a look around. Last night was the first night since she'd moved in that she had not slept in the house. She felt like she needed to check every nook and cranny to make sure everything had gone well.

"Thanks so much for handling things while I was out," Marie said.

"Of course. You missed nothing. Benjamin will be fixing the gutters today, the new stone for the flowerbeds will be here in two days, and the house is still standing." They had come into the dining room, where Posey now swept her arms around dramatically. "Now. It is time for you to eat."

At first, Marie didn't understand what she was seeing. There were about a dozen different breakfast pastries on the table, and half a loaf of what looked and smelled like banana bread.

"What is all this?" Marie asked.

"I've been wanting to try out some new breakfast pastries. I didn't think you'd want me using guests as guinea pigs, so you get the honor. Would you like some coffee to go with the taste test?"

Marie knew she shouldn't because it would ruin any hope of catching a nap. But she could smell it, freshly brewed in the kitchen, and could not turn it down. "Yes, please."

She sat down, studying the variety of breakfast treats Posey had set out for her. Some were easy to recognize; there was what looked like a cheese Danish, and a beignet with a red-colored sauce. Others were a little harder to identify.

Posey came in with the coffee and set it down in front of Marie. She then instantly slid one of the waiting plates in front of her. "This one is my vanilla almond scone," she said proudly. "It might be my favorite out of everything you're about to try."

Marie picked the scone up and took a bite. The taste of it made her feel like melting. It also made her wonder if all of Posey's work was worth it. With no guests scheduled to arrive in the next few days, Marie wasn't so sure Posey would ever get the chance to cook such delicious foods for June Manor again.

"Posey, this is amazing!"

"I thought so, too," she said, sliding a glass of water in front of her. "Now clean off that taste and try this." She then slid a cylindrical-looking pastry in front of her that looked to be stuffed with cherries.

Marie bit into it and again, could have melted into her seat. "Posey," she said through a mouthful of bread, cream, and cherries. "This is unreal…"

But it wasn't the end of it, not by any stretch of the imagination. Next came the beignet with raspberry sauce, then a coffee cream muffin. Marie could have gone through every plate Posey had prepared even though her stomach was already indicating it was getting close to full.

But she didn't get that chance. Just as Posey was sliding a thick slice of banana walnut bread in front of her, the little bell over the front door rang out as someone entered the house. In the past few weeks or so, it was a sound that had come to get her just as excited as the notification bell on her phone that let her know a reservation had been made online. Usually it was just Posey or Benjamin, but she always held out the hope that it might be another potential guest coming to book a room.

"Be right back," Marie said, getting up from the chair, quite sad to be leaving all the food behind.

She walked through the sitting room and could see a man standing by the check-in desk, waiting patiently and taking in the sights. She was happy to see that he was smiling. As she approached him, she quickly looked him over. He was middle-aged and dressed nicely, wearing a button-down shirt and a pair of slacks. But he didn't look stuffy; he looked like the sort of man who dressed this way all the time and was quite comfortable in it.

"Does it always smell so delicious in here?" the man asked.

"Sometimes," Marie said. "My cook has me sampling some new pastries, so that's what you're smelling right now."

"Lucky you." He smiled broadly and then gestured around the foyer. "You really do have an amazing place here."

"Thanks. And we're working to make it better."

"Ah, well, that's good to hear. It makes my reason for visiting all that much more meaningful." He shook his head, as if ashamed of himself, and then sighed. "Forgive me. Where are my manners? Ms. Fortune, my name is Avery Decker." He extended his hand for a shake and added: "And I'm here to do you an incredible favor."

"And what favor is that?" Marie asked, shaking his hand.

"I'm here to buy this property from you."

CHAPTER FIVE

Marie jerked her hand back quickly. She was pretty sure this had come off as rude, but she didn't care. She'd already dealt with one pushy real estate agent before she had even properly moved in—a rather presumptuous and snotty lady named Stacy Hamlett. And now here was another one, likely wanting to snatch the place up following her failings in going public with June Manor being potentially haunted.

"That's not really much of a favor," Marie said. "I'm not at all interested in selling. This was my great-aunt's house, and it was given to me. And, as you can see, I'm trying to run a business here."

"Yes, and I've heard all about your business," Avery Decker said. "The coastal bed-and-breakfast that's sort of haunted, but not really."

"Well, that's not quite fair now, is it?"

Decker shrugged but it was clear that he was not sorry for what he had said. It was a gesture that made Marie pretty sure Decker was used to speaking to people any way he wanted—and usually getting his way as a result.

"Here's the deal," Decker said. "I'm the former owner of a construction company that did quite well in the area about twenty years ago. Over the past five years or so, I've become something of a property developer and I've had my eye on this house for quite some time. The former owner wasn't a fan of me purchasing it, either."

Marie smiled at the picture of Aunt June verbally telling this man to kick rocks. "So what you're saying is you buy houses, flip them, and sell them."

"That's a crude and oversimplified explanation, but yes...that's the core of it. And of course, I'm willing to pay handsomely for the place."

"Not interested."

"No?" Decker said. He was grinning at her, as if he were ready to play ball and could do it all day. "You sure? Let's not paint the picture prettier than it is. It doesn't seem like your business is doing too well. Let me take this burden off your hands."

"It's not a burden," Marie said, doing her best not to lose her temper.

"Go ahead…name your price," Decker went on, undeterred. "I understand sentimentality for sure, but I also understand money and business. So for real. Name your price."

Marie placed her elbows on the check-in desk and looked him directly in the eye. She wanted to let him know she wasn't like others he apparently bullied. "Ten million dollars," she said.

Decker laughed out loud and slapped his knee. "Now, Ms. Fortune, you have to know that's absolutely ridiculous."

"It's no more ridiculous than a complete stranger coming into my home and business, thinking he's doing me a favor by buying a house I have no interest in selling."

"Now, Ms. Fortune, you and I can make a very nice payday off of this if—"

"Not interested."

"Well, I already know of four potential buyers that have deep pock—"

"*Not. Interested.*" She took a deep breath, trying to keep the rage away. "That said, I have other things I need to tend to. So, if you'll excuse me…"

She knew Decker was getting the point, but refusing to go away so easily. When Marie then extended her hand and pointed at the door, he finally got moving. He grinned and shook his head. As he made his way to the door, he called out over his shoulder. "Just remember my name in six months when you're drowning in debt and the place is going belly up. You might be able to convince me to buy."

He closed the door immediately afterward, making sure he got the last word in. When she was by herself, she said a silent *Oh my God* and placed her hand to her mouth. She had never been so rude to someone in her life. Sure, Avery Decker had deserved it, but it was an alien feeling to her.

She stood there a moment longer, staring at the front door and trying to get herself under control. Just as she stepped away from the check-in desk, ready to head back into the dining room and give more thoughts on Posey's new offerings, she heard the sound of heavy, rapid footsteps somewhere upstairs.

She instantly thought of ghosts, but these footfalls were somehow more present. More real. And as they drew closer to the stairs and then down them, she shook ideas of the supernatural away. It was just Benjamin. Only, he looked a little spooked and confused.

"Where is your guest?" Benjamin asked.

"I kicked him out. You okay, Benjamin?"

"Yes. But…I think there is something upstairs you should see."

Her anger was still present from having dealt with Avery Decker and she had to choke it down even further to keep from snapping at Benjamin. Instead, her remark came out passive-aggressively. "Something else I'm going to need to shell out more money for?"

"No, nothing like that. Just…come see."

He started back up the stairs and she followed after him, not sure what to expect. Benjamin usually only bothered her with questions and updates when it was important. She'd told him from the start that every little decision did not need to be run by her—that she trusted his judgment and experience.

He led her to the back bedroom along the upstairs hallway, the same bedroom where he was replacing the old, tattered carpet in the closet. When she followed him into the room, she found the closet door open. He had not yet started tearing up the carpet from what she could tell.

"So what is it?" she asked.

"I was in the closet, starting to tear up the old carpet and found something weird against the wall. Go have a look."

She noted that he was standing a good distance away from the closet. He did not look scared, but definitely uncertain about something. She was slightly irritated that he wasn't just coming out and telling her what it was, but there was also an exciting element of mystery to it all.

She walked into the closet. It was a modest closet, a bit bigger than a typical coat closet, but not spacious enough to fully stretch her arms out. She could extend her hands to both sides and not touch either wall, but just barely. She looked down at the floor and saw where Benjamin had started pulling the carpet up in the back corner. Seeing this, she also spotted the oddity he had mentioned.

About three inches off of the corner, there was a straight line that had been etched into the wall. As she knelt down by it and looked, she saw that it was more than an etching—it looked like a straight crack that had intentionally been placed there. It ran up about six inches and then disappeared. The way in which it had just winked out of existence made her realize that the wall was not painted; it was covered in wallpaper. How had she never noticed that before?

27

"Did you know this was wallpapered?" she asked.

"No," Benjamin said, still keeping his distance.

"What do you think it is?"

"I think it is a door. I didn't want to tear the wallpaper without your permission."

Marie didn't even have to think about it. She reached out and tore at the wallpaper. It came up easier than she expected. It tore several times as she ripped it off, but it was done quickly. And the more she tore off, the more Benjamin's suspicion proved to be true.

When all of the wallpaper was removed, there was indeed a door behind it—hidden for countless years, waiting to be opened.

CHAPTER SIX

The door was thin and rather bland, made of simple untreated wood. The hinges looked as if they had been hastily put on. Rather than a knob, there was a circular handle hanging down. It reminded Marie of something from a castle or dungeon.

Marie wasn't sure if she should be excited or terrified. Clearly, someone had wanted this room hidden. Sure, it had been concealed rather lazily with wallpaper, but still...it had been hidden. She took a moment to figure out if she should even consider opening it.

"You going to open it?" Benjamin asked. He was in the closet doorway now, peering in.

"I think we have to," Marie said, making her decision. "I mean...it's a hidden room in my great-aunt's house."

She reached for the circular handle, lifted it up, and pulled.

The door creaked but came open easily. Even before it was completely open, the smell of dust and neglect came wafting out. Marie felt the need to sneeze immediately. When the door was fully opened, Marie found herself looking into a small room. It was about a quarter of the size of the bedroom she had just been standing in. She guessed it to be about ten feet by eight feet. There were no windows and, from what she could see, no lights. The room had only been moderately finished; the walls were just boards nailed into the frame of the house and the floor looked to be only a few thick sheets of plywood that had been bolted to one another and then also nailed into the frame.

Sitting in the center of the room was a small table, built with scrap wood and a sheen of weak polish. It, like the chair that sat tucked beneath one of the sides, looked very old. There was a book on the table and, next to it, a partially burned candle sitting in a brass holder. The book and the candle were both coated in a thick layer of dust.

Marie stepped into the room and went to the table. She nearly reached out and picked the book up but felt strange even thinking of disturbing its placement. She drew her hand back at the last moment. The book was a little larger than a modern hardback book and each page had two columns. She approached the book, her eyes instantly drawn to the dusty pages.

A shout from downstairs made Marie jump back from the table and stifle a little scream.

"Hey, Marie!" It was Posey's voice. And though it was cheerful as always, it had still sent a spike of fear right through Marie's heart. Especially as she stood in the hidden room, her eyes on the mysterious book. She wanted to go to it, to see what she could find out about it. But she knew if she set her eyes on it, it would be impossible to look away. So she instead turned around and gave her full attention to Posey's call.

"Yeah?" she called out, slowly backing out of the small room.

"Someone just pulled up. Maybe a guest. He sure does look like the type that Brendan attracted here for a while."

The act of shouting back and forth throughout the house was causing her head to ache. And though she was enamored with the room and did not want to leave, she also knew that she had to treat every guest as special. It was a rule she hoped to always keep, but it was especially true right now, as she was barely hanging on financially.

She forced herself away from the doorway and headed out of the room. As she left, Benjamin asked, "What should I do? You still want me to replace the carpet?"

"Not right now," she said. "Let's hold off on that."

She ran downstairs, hoping to get there to greet the guest before they came in. But she was still preoccupied with the discovery of the secret room and the book inside. And even beyond that, she was already growing giddy with the idea that there could easily be many more surprises just waiting to be found.

She got downstairs just as the man was coming in through the front door. As Marie took her place behind the check-in desk, she took in the sight of one of the most peculiar-looking men Marie had ever seen. If it weren't for his jet black hair, she would have thought he was an albino. His skin was nearly chalk white, but not in any way that looked entirely natural. It almost looked as if the color had been powdered on, but as he came closer to the desk, Marie saw that this was not the case. His hair was rather long, combed back tightly on his head so that the length of it made a sort of ducktail shape behind his shoulders. He wore a pair of very dark and narrow sunglasses that matched his black jacket, T-shirt, and jeans. A black driver's cap perched on his head tied the whole ensemble together in a dark little bow.

"Welcome to June Manor," she said brightly. "How can I help you?"

"Do you have any vacancies?" he asked. His voice was thin and slightly British-sounding. He lips were also incredibly thin; when his mouth was closed, his lips were barely visible and looked like a thin pencil line along his jaw.

"We do," Marie said. "We actually are wide open right now. So you could have your pick of the rooms."

"Excellent," he said, without any real emotion. "I require a room for three days. Perhaps longer, as I do not know how long I will be in the area."

"Certainly. I will make sure you—"

"Now, before we book anything, I do have a request. I will be in my room most of the time I am here. I require the utmost privacy. No knocking on my door for anything."

He didn't sound rude, but it *felt* rude. But that was okay with Marie. She supposed a guest you hardly ever saw was the easiest sort of guest.

"We can make sure you get all the quiet and privacy you need," Marie assured him. "Would you like an ocean view?"

"I do not care about the view. Only privacy. And nothing on the ground floor."

As she thought of placing him into an upstairs room, her mind turned to the secret room she and Benjamin had just discovered. She would be sure to place this new guest all the way at the other end of the hallway, right by the stairs.

Marie started typing the information into her spreadsheet, using the laptop at the little desk. "And what name will this be under?"

"Is a name truly necessary? I shall be paying in cash."

"Well, I just need it for my records." She was not irritated with him (not yet, anyway) but was at a loss as far as how to speak to him.

"Very well. My name is Atticus Winslow." He said this rather begrudgingly as he pulled a wad of money from his pocket. As he flipped through it, taking out a few bills, Marie saw that they were all hundreds. "How much?" he asked.

"For three days and nights, that comes to four hundred and twenty dollars."

31

Atticus Winslow counted off five of the bills and handed them to her. "Keep the remainder. We will either push it toward more days if needed, or I'll include it with gratuity."

"Thank you. Now, do you need help with your bags?"

"I have no bags."

"Oh...I thought you were staying multiple days."

"Indeed," he said, looking at her expectantly.

Marie, still puzzled by this man, handed him the key to the first bedroom at the east end of the upstairs hallway. While he did not snatch it, he took it in a way that made her feel as if she was wasting his time. It did seem rude, but she thought of the wad of one-hundred-dollar bills he had just pulled out. Atticus Winslow was apparently accustomed to being waited on and pampered in certain ways.

"Just let me know if you need anything." She turned her eyes toward the stairs and again thought about the hidden room. What if Atticus saw it? What if Benjamin was still standing in that bedroom, marveling at their discovery?

After she watched him go, she saw Posey step into the foyer. "I heard all of that," she said quietly. "Seems rather strange, doesn't he?"

"That's putting it mildly," Marie said. "It's been a very strange fifteen minutes or so and I—"

Her cell phone rang and, as usual, she answered it at once. She grimaced, realizing she had done so without giving any sort of apology or indication to Posey. But Posey understood, having already turned back for the dining room.

"June Manor, this is Marie speaking."

"Marie?" It was a woman's voice. She sounded tired and maybe a little agitated.

"Yes...that's me."

"Hi, Marie. This is Anna Grace...and I want to know what the hell you did to my house last night."

CHAPTER SEVEN

"I'm sorry…I don't understand."

She walked down the hall, toward her bedroom. Based on the way this conversation had started, it was not something she wanted Posey to hear.

"Well, just what I asked," Mrs. Grace said. "I don't know what you did…but it's different here now. It's unmistakable."

"What kind of *different*?" Marie asked.

"Oh, it's amazing. I walked back into the place this morning and it almost felt like someone had come in overnight and cleaned the place. I can feel it in the air. Just walking around the house, it *feels* different. Whatever you did…thank you."

"I'm glad I could help." But even as she said it, Marie felt like a fraud. She'd done nothing. It had all been Boo. The only thing Marie had done was give Boo a ride over to Bloom Gardens and Rest.

"Can I ask you something, though?" Mrs. Grace asked.

"Of course."

"Have you always been able to do it?"

Marie frowned. That question alone made her realize that the deeper she went into this, the more she was going to have to lie. She did not like to lie and, more to the point, had never been exceptionally good at it.

"I honestly don't know," she said. "If I did, I wasn't aware of it. This sort of just came about recently. Something I discovered at my own bed-and-breakfast."

"Well, I'm a woman true to my word. I'll gladly pay you. Ms. Fortune, I swear, it's like I'm standing in a new house. Now…if I can just get the word out to the public that it's a new place…"

Marie couldn't help but smile. "If you figure that out, let me know. I'm sort of in the same boat, as you know."

The women went over payment details, and Marie once again felt almost guilty. She was being paid a large lump sum of money for something her dog had done. It made her wonder exactly what Brendan had been thinking when he'd originally told Mrs. Grace the first white lie—that he knew this lady in Port Bliss who was something of a ghost exterminator.

When she ended the call, Marie wasn't sure how to feel. Sure, there was the guilt of being untruthful, but there was also the relief of the money—and that Boo's little trick at June Manor had not been a fluke. Apparently, she had a dog that was capable of chasing ghosts away.

She walked back to the check-in desk and glanced up the stairs. Thinking of the newly discovered small room and the weird book it held, as well as Atticus Winslow's arrival, Marie suddenly felt like her world was starting to spiral out of control. The odd thing was, though, that it was a *good* sort of chaos. She was just having some trouble wrapping her mind around it all.

She headed back toward the dining room, hoping to properly apologize to Posey for dipping out on her. Honestly, she only wanted to do it so she could then turn her full attention to the secret room hidden in the closet upstairs. But halfway down the hall, her phone rang yet again. She rolled her eyes and took a deep breath. What else could this day possibly have in store for her?

When she saw the name on the display, she smiled. And she was slightly uneasy with how genuine the smile was. She answered the call, putting on a playfully annoyed tone.

"Brendan Peck," she said. "What do you want?"

"Marie! You survived!"

"I did, smartass. No thanks to you."

"That hurts. But…I take it Operation Bloom Gardens and Rest was a success?"

"It was. I just got a call from her, thanking me. She seemed very surprised and grateful. But I feel awful for lying to Mrs. Grace—letting her think I'm the one responsible for…for *cleansing* her house."

"Well, you sort of did, right? Boo is your dog. He follows you around, obeys you and all that. So I don't think it's wrong if you take the credit for it."

"You're far too good at skewing the truth. You know that?"

"Yeah, it's an occupational hazard."

"How was your convention?"

He seemed surprised that she asked, but was happy to answer. She listened to him while she walked and then the tables were turned. He asked for details about what went down at Bloom Gardens and Rest.

And as she recounted it all, she found that she *was* sort of excited to walk through it, to describe what had happened step by step.

It made her think she was almost on the believer side of the paranormal fence.

She nearly told him about the secret room upstairs, and the book. She figured he would absolutely flip over that book—which was why she didn't tell him. She wanted to fully understand what the room was all about first.

"Well, listen. Sometime in the next few weeks, I might be heading to Bangor. There's a Stephen King convention sorta thing up there and I'm something of an expert on *The Shining*, so..."

"That's an actual thing?"

"Have you *seen* the sort of fans I attract?"

"I have. Hey, by the way, do you happen to know anyone named Atticus Winslow?"

"Doesn't ring a bell. Sounds like a vampire name."

Recalling the man's appearance, Marie realized it did sort of fit. "Anyway...Bangor. You were saying?"

"On my way through, I'd like to come by and say hi. Can you book me a room for two weeks from now?"

"That would be great," she said. And then, thinking of her newly discovered room, she said, "And I think I have just the right room for you."

"That sounds a little foreboding."

"Good. We can—"

Her phone dinged in her ear, giving her an alert sound she wasn't overly familiar with. "Are you kidding me?" she said to no one in particular.

"Something wrong?" Brendan asked.

"No, my phone has just been going off today like crazy. "One second..."

She looked at her phone and saw that a reminder alert had popped up. When she read it, her heart went cold for a moment. She had set the reminder a while back—almost two years ago—but had totally forgotten about it until now. Seeing it, any happiness or joy she had managed to scrape up during the morning went slowly melting away.

"Brendan, I need to go. But I'll see you in two weeks, right?"

He responded, but she barely heard him. They ended the call and Marie looked back at the reminder. Reading it, she couldn't help but

35

think that it was perfect timing—that this reminder would come to date while she was a resident of Port Bliss.

It did not make her *sad* per se, but it definitely soured her mood. She read the simple Reminder message over and over again, trying to understand how it was making her feel. The reminder alert read:

Today, Mom has been missing for 25 years.

CHAPTER EIGHT

Marie walked out onto the pier that sat off of West Tide Avenue, still thinking about the hidden room back at June Manor. She regretted not exploring it right away, but she also knew that committing herself to it would have distracted her from this little trip—a trip she had put off for far too long. She would check out the room when she got back. For now…well, she had to peek into her past for a moment.

The pier on West Tide Avenue sat on the western rim of Port Bliss. It was two in the afternoon, and there was only one other person on the pier, casting a fishing line into the water. There was nothing special about the pier at first glance; it was an offshoot of a little wooden walkway that connected a few little beach shops and a bait and tackle center for anglers. A few waiting boats bobbed lazily in the water to the sides. But, according to Great-Aunt June, it was also the place Marie's mother had last been seen.

Of course, that was according to Aunt June. As far as anyone else was concerned, the story revolving around Abigail Fortune had her driving out of Port Bliss, never to be seen again. But Marie figured the pier was a better communal place rather than driving randomly out of town.

Marie had known about June's pier theory, saying that a few people had seen her mother standing idly on it on the same day she allegedly left town. But she had somehow managed to push the knowledge to the back of her mind after coming to Port Bliss. She had been too focused on the business and then, oddly enough, on all matter of supernatural mumbo jumbo. And besides that, she typically tried to avoid just about everything pertaining to her mother. Coming out here for any sort of sentimental purpose would be a roundabout admission that her mother's disappearance had bothered her more than she had let on for most of her life.

But two years ago, when she had set the alarm in her phone for the twenty-five-year disappearance of her mother, she'd done so because she figured there was a point in everyone's life where they had to face their past. It seemed especially fitting now that she had achieved her lifelong dream (by no means of her own) and owned a bed-and-breakfast in Port Bliss. The town had been one of her mother's favorite places, which made the fact that she had seemingly disappeared from it years ago fitting on a morbid way.

Marie came to the end of the little pier and looked out at the ocean. Leaning against the rail, she could feel the force of the ocean beneath her. She watched the waves come in and crash along the beach, some escaping from her sight beneath the pier.

"Okay," she said to the sea. "I'm here. I don't know why, exactly, but here I am."

When the words were out of her mouth, she realized she was talking to her mother. It made her feel weird at first—and maybe even a little nutty—but she found that she wanted to keep talking. She figured it was no different than someone visiting the graveside of a loved one, talking to them in a strange form of therapy or connection.

"You know, it might be a lot easier to talk to you like this if I knew if you were alive or dead," she went on. "You know, the police never actually came out and said they believed you were dead somewhere. But it's been long enough now—twenty-five years, to be exact—to go ahead and declare you legally dead. Although, technically, I think it's been more like twenty-four years and eleven months. I don't know if that matters or not. I honestly don't remember when you went missing. Aunt June told me at some point, but I don't remember, and…"

She hesitated for a moment, her heart leaning into this odd form of communication. Maybe it was the waves, or the bright sun reflecting from the water, but she *wanted* to speak to her mother in this way. With each word, she felt…well, she wasn't quite sure. But it seemed to be helping to release some of the weight and worry that had accumulated on her shoulders ever since moving to Port Bliss.

"Anyway, so I'm living in Aunt June's house. Maybe you know that. If you *are* dead and there's a Heaven, I'm sure she's found you by now. So I'm running a bed-and-breakfast out of her house and it's been interesting to say the least. Just this morning, I found this weird hidden room. And it may or may not have been haunted at one point but I have this dog that maybe ran the ghosts—if that's what they were—off and—"

She stopped here, letting out a nervous chuckle. God, it did all sound crazy. She took a deep, steadying breath and went on. "Business is struggling, but I've at least gotten some stories out of it, as you can see. Stories Aunt June would love. Stories about ghosts and strange dogs. But hey, I've only had the cops show up once, over a very strange hot air balloon incident, and that's just—"

She stopped here, hung up on something she'd said. She thought over her last words and an idea occurred to her. How had she never thought of it before?

I've only had the cops show up once…

Something like excitement stirred in her heart and she slowly stepped away from the pier rail. Still looking at the white caps of the waves coming in, she said, "It's been real, Mom. But I think there's something I need to do."

And with that, she walked back down the pier. By the time she passed by the man who was fishing, she was walking quite fast and wondering what her old friend Deputy Miles was up to.

***

The Winscott County Police Department looked almost as quaint as every other building within the Port Bliss city limits. The parking lot was relatively empty, as Marie had expected; Port Bliss did not really seem like the sort of place where the police were called out on pressing calls time and time again. When Marie walked into the station, she found it welcoming and bright. A large lobby-type area made up the front of the building, most of the area squared off with desks and a few cubicles against the far wall.

A plump and cheerful lady sat at the first desk, the largest in the room and clearly serving as the reception area. "Hey to you," she said, her cheer so thick Marie could feel it clinging to her like a cobweb. "What can we do for you today?"

"It's a long shot, I know," Marie said. "But is Deputy Miles in?"

"You know what, I think he *is* back in his office, actually. Let me buzz him and make sure. Can I tell him who's asking?"

"Marie Fortune."

The woman nodded and grinned, making Marie wonder if the receptionist had somehow picked her name up over the past few weeks—particularly during the few days she had been eyed as a potential murder suspect.

Marie waited as the receptionist picked up the phone and dialed up the office in question. She made no attempt to remain quiet as she said:

"Just making sure you were in there. There's a Miss Marie Fortune out here, asking to speak with you. Can I send her back?" There was a slight pause before the receptionist hung up. She then pushed a button under her desk to open the small half gate that allowed visitors back behind into the office area that Marie had always thought of as "the bullpen."

"Third office down the hall on the right," the receptionist said, waving her through.

Marie headed through the little swinging gate and back through the maze of desks and cubicles. When she came to the hallway and looked at the doors on the right, the third one down opened. Deputy Miles was standing there, holding it open for her. He wore the same thin smile she'd always seen on his face. He never looked happy, but never angry or irritated, either. He seemed to be in a neutral state, just like the hair at his temples that seemed to have settled on a shade somewhere between his natural black and the gray that seemed hesitant to start taking over.

"Ms. Fortune, it's a pleasure to see you," he said. "Come on in."

When she passed by him and into his office, Marie felt a little odd. After all, he'd done his best to remain on her side throughout the case of Alfred Ryker's mysterious death. She didn't know the man particularly well, but she felt that they'd gone through a lot together. It had been Deputy Miles who had informed her of Aunt June's passing, and then had to eye her as a suspect in Ryker's death.

So when he genuinely smiled at her when he took his seat behind his desk, she was glad to see it. "You been doing well?" he asked.

"Better than the last time you saw me, that's for sure. Personally, anyway. Business is still sort of struggling."

"Sorry to hear that. But I think if you give it time, things will smooth over and you'll do just fine. But I digress. I am not a career coach by any stretch of the imagination. What can I do for you today?"

"Well, I don't remember how much you know about my past. I know we discussed a bit of it when you informed me that Aunt June had died. Anyway, I was wondering if you had access to an old case. Like *old*. Twenty-five years or so."

Miles nodded, his mouth set in a thin line. "Your mother, right?"

"Right...but how did you know?"

"June poked her head in every now and again to check up on a case about a relative of hers over the years. Granted, I never worked directly with her, so I'm not aware of *all* of the details. But when I was eyeballing you when all the Ryker stuff went down, I made the connection. The woman she was wanting to check up on was your mother, right? Abigail Fortune. Went missing about twenty-five years ago, last seen here in Port Bliss."

"Yeah, that would be her. And yes…that's the case I'm wondering about."

"It's *technically* an open case, and there's not too much I can tell you even with you being the daughter. However, if it's been twenty-five years, that changes things."

"Because she'd be declared legally dead if I chose to make the declaration, right?"

"Right."

"And what happens then?"

"Even if you do decide *not* to declare her legally dead, the case would officially become a cold case. Honestly, it's pretty much already been a cold case for the last five years or so. I haven't dug through the files myself, but I do know it hasn't seen much activity over the past decade. And the little bit of activity it *did* see was only the result of June checking in."

"And is there any way I can see the files?"

"If you sign a few papers, we can get out the preliminary reports from the start of the investigation. But anything regarding behind-the-scenes-type material is harder to get. But I'm pretty sure, in your mother's case, there really wasn't all that much to go on in the first place."

"I understand. But in the meantime, would you mind letting me fill out those forms?"

"Not at all," he said. "I can have Nancy at reception hand them to you on your way out."

"Thanks so much. You know, I think I might—"

Her phone had interrupted her so much in the past few days that it didn't surprise her when it did right there and then, in Deputy Miles's office. Once again, she did not recognize the number on the display.

"I'm so sorry," she said. "Do you mind?"

"Not at all," he said. "In fact, I'll go talk to Nancy and get those forms for you. Take your time."

He stood up from his desk and made his exit. As soon as he closed the door behind him, Marie answered the call. "This is Marie with June Manor, how can I help you?"

"Marie Fortune, right?" a male voice on the other end said.

"That's me. What can I do for you?"

"Ms. Fortune, I was given your name by Anna Grace, over at Bloom Gardens and Rest. She says you helped her with her...well, her *problem*. And I was really hoping you might help me, too."

Marie felt her mind lock up for a moment. It was similar to a certain word being right on the tip of her tongue but her brain would simply not formulate the word. Was she hearing this man correctly? She was pretty sure she was. Or was it maybe a joke? Had Brendan Peck reached out to someone to have some fun at her expense?

"Ms. Fortune, are you there?"

"Yes, I'm here. Just...thinking."

That was an understatement. If this man was for real and she took him up on it, what sort of reputation might this give her? If her name was already getting around about this sort of thing, what would it look like if it kept going? How would it affect things at June Manor?

Then again, she recalled Ms. Grace's bright and cheerful voice. Marie had helped her and it changed her life. And it was *that* thought that obliterated everything else, making it easy for her to eventually ask: "Well, what sort of problem are we talking about?"

"Voices, mainly. And sometimes I can feel someone sort of tickling the back of my neck. I've tried ignoring it for years now but I think it's getting worse. I didn't even know there were people that could do what you did for Mrs. Grace but when she told me how you helped her, I had to call. So...do you think you can help?"

"I don't know," she said. "These things take some time. I don't know if I could even make it through something like that so soon after Ms. Grace's house."

"Please," he said. "As you might imagine, there isn't anyone else I can call for something like this. I tried the church one time, believe it or not. Hoping they could maybe come by and do an exorcism on the house or something, but they sort of laughed me off. And quite frankly, I am starting to feel like I might be losing my mind."

Her heart broke for him but the truth of the matter was that his accounts were terrifying. His descriptions were certainly horrifying—perhaps scarier than anything she had heard of ever since her life had become centered around such stories. She couldn't help but wonder if this instance might be too much for Boo. Or, for that matter, if he was even capable of doing his little trick twice in such a short span of time.

Marie took a moment to think about it. Yes, she had been terrified at the beginning of the job at Mrs. Grace's house. But everything had worked out okay and Boo had proven his talents. Besides…if she had the opportunity to help someone else, why not take it?

She grabbed a pen and a nearby Post-it stack from Deputy Miles's desk and said: "What's the address?"

CHAPTER NINE

As Marie pulled into the driveway of the address the man had given her on the phone, a thought occurred to her. Including June Manor, this house would be the third allegedly haunted one she'd encountered since moving to Port Bliss a little less than two months ago. It made her wonder if reports of hauntings were more widespread than most people thought—and, as such, if it was why people like Brendan Peck were constantly enamored with the supernatural even when evidence was so hard to come by.

This house, owned by a sixty-one-year-old gentleman named Wallace Jackson, was located just a single block away from the beach in another coastal town called Salt Bay. Forty minutes away from Port Bliss, it looked almost the same as Marie's new hometown but not quite as quaint and trendy. The businesses looked older, but in a nostalgic sort of way. It was the kind of little town that, for just a moment, made her feel as if her car was a time machine and she had gone back about fifteen or twenty years.

Wallace's house had the same effect. Still, it felt rather familiar when she pulled her car into the driveway, parking behind Wallace's old pickup truck. The house was not quite as big as June Manor, but did have some of the same qualities; it was regal-looking but in need of repair; it had a creepy vibe at first but then revealed more of its unique qualities the closer she go to it; it sat very close to the beach but looked out of place in the beachside community.

As she took in the sight of the house, Wallace Jackson came through the front door, apparently anxious to meet her. He was a tall, older man who walked with his back slightly hunched. He wore an old, rugged cap bearing the name of a company she instantly assumed had something to do with cars or oil or some sort of power equipment; she wasn't sure why, she just got than impression.

She got out of the car, Boo trailing along beside her. He looked quizzically at the house. She wasn't sure, but it was almost as if he already knew why they were there.

"Sorry, boy," she said. "Most dogs get to play fetch, not this sort of thing. Though I guess you are sort of fetching ghosts, right?"

He pricked an ear up, as if to indicate he'd heard this, but did not find it funny. They walked to the porch, where Wallace was waiting. He looked back and forth between them, as if he had been expecting them to look quite different.

"Mr. Jackson?" she asked as she came up to the porch. Like the rest of the house, it needed some upkeep but was also rather beautiful.

"Just Wallace, please. Thanks for coming out, Ms. Fortune." He looked at her with a strange expression, the same way Boo sometimes did when he wasn't quite sure how to approach her. His dark eyes looked worried and speculative.

"Something wrong?" Marie asked.

"No," Wallace said. "It's just that…well, don't take this the wrong way. But I thought you'd be sort of weird-looking, you know? Like one of those goth kids or something, all obsessed with death."

She chuckled and shook her head. "No. I'm pretty normal. Only, I do bring my dog along on these little adventures. He's sort of like a therapy dog, I guess. Helps me deal with the fright of it all. I hope it's okay that he's here?"

"Oh sure. I had a dog myself up until two years ago and he spent most of his time curled up in the den." He shrugged, as if he wasn't sure how to proceed with the conversation, and then waved her in. "Well, come on inside and I'll do my best to explain things."

The interior of the house honestly made Marie feel slightly jealous. There were very few hints of the gothic vibe in Wallace's house. Instead, it looked like a very large study. The furniture all looked antique and refined. The floorboards creaked pleasantly under her feet as he led her into the large living room. There were books everywhere. A record player sat on a long bench in the back of the room, aligned beside a shelf filled with records. The ceilings were high, but not *too* high, and the place smelled like the inside of a new paperback book.

"This is where most of the activity happens," Wallace said. "I'll gladly show you around the rest of the house if you want to see it, but almost every single thing that has happened has occurred here."

"What sorts of things are you talking about?" Marie asked.

"Murmurs. Whispers. Every now and then there will be footsteps and, like I said earlier, like someone sort of plucking at the back of my neck. A recent case was with a fellow that was staying here, in the

45

upstairs bedroom. From time to time, I rent out two of the rooms as a sort of bed-and-breakfast—just a listing on Airbnb, nothing fancy. But two days ago, this young man swore he woke up early in the morning with something heavy sitting on his chest. He said he couldn't see anything, but he was pinned to the bed."

"Oh my God." She'd only heard about such things a few times in her life. Once was on an old episode of *Unsolved Mysteries* she'd seen as a kid. The other was just hearing random conversation in passing when Brendan Peck and some of his fans had been staying at June Manor.

"He was terrified. Ran out of here as fast as he could. Damn near left his luggage."

"Have you ever experienced anything like that?"

"Nothing that bad, no. Just the little tickles at the back of the neck I was telling you about."

"Are they trying to scare you?" Marie asked. She felt like an idiot conducting this sort of interview. She really wished Brandon were here. He'd know exactly what to say, exactly what to ask. She cursed at herself internally for not calling him beforehand, but there had only been two hours between receiving the call, heading back to June Manor to pack a few things and get things squared away, and pulling up into Wallace's driveway.

"I don't know. What I do know is that when I was married, my wife swore the ghosts—or whatever they were—would tickle her feet at night, or watch her while she undressed. Nothing menacing, but just enough to make your life really inconvenient. And now, really, it's just the whispering. But it's constant…like bees buzzing. And there are days where I think it's going to drive me crazy. I just don't know how much longer I can take it."

"And you're sure it's voices?" Marie asked.

"Yes, I'm sure," he snapped. He then frowned and rubbed his brow has if shoving thoughts back into his head. "I'm sorry. But I've seen a therapist about this, and he used to ask me the same thing. He said it's an old house that gets the brunt of coastal winds so there are lots of odd sounds I might hear as a result. And to his credit, he's right. Sometimes the winds off the sea hit this old house and the wind—especially when it comes through the attic—makes some hellacious noise. But not voices. I've lived in this house for three years now, and I know the noises it makes."

46

"Where'd you live before this?"

"New York. Little town called Willings. Moved away because it was just too close to the city. And the wife and I always wanted a small house somewhere near the coast…just not in New York."

"So, these voices…do they say anything that you can make out?"

"Sometimes. And it's always either very sad-sounding, or menacing. Never just conversational. One of the voices is a woman that I've heard say the same thing at least a dozen times. 'I miss Adam. Where's Adam?' And then there's this older voice that I think is telling jokes to himself. I always catch him at the tail end of a joke and then his laughs. But there's one voice, this somber male voice that says something like: 'Your life is a trap and your mother was ugly.'"

"That's…specific," Marie said.

"I know it doesn't sound like a lot…like nothing too scary," Wallace said. "But over several years, those voices always whispering…"

She could see the pain in his eyes, the fear that no one was going to understand him. He also looked rather ashamed, perhaps embarrassed that it had come to this. She could only imagine what he might feel like if he discovered that it was not her that would be doing the work here, but the dog he had so graciously allowed into his home.

"I understand," she said, though she wasn't sure she did at all. "And we'll do our best to make sure you have a home you'll feel safe in."

"Thank you. I'll pay you, of course. Mrs. Grace told me what she paid you and I can't quite match that and—"

"Don't worry about that for now. We'll get it figured out."

"Thank you. Mrs. Grace also said she wasn't there when you worked on her house," Wallace said. "So if it's okay, I think I'm going to find some place to stay for the night."

"Well, you know," she said, with a smile, "I can recommend a good bed-and-breakfast."

***

Boo did a few quick laps around the house but always came back to the living room. He seemed unsettled about something, not his usual casual self. In the two hours since Wallace Jackson had left, Boo had not rested at her feet a single time. On more than one occasion, Marie noticed him standing at attention, his head cocked to the side, his tail

47

slightly stiff. But he had shown no signs of aggression the entire time. Not even a single low-throated growl.

Marie had taken a quick tour of the house and found the rest just as gorgeous as the den area. It was clearly old, but in a classy sort of way. It reminded her of libraries and smaller local-type museums. It was the sort of house that would be perfect with a woodfire going on a snowy winter's day. Yet, as she settled back down in the den, she realized that Wallace did not own a TV. She supposed he didn't need one with all the books he had.

She scanned the titles that were all around the living room—crammed into five different bookshelves and all over (and even under) the coffee table. She selected a photography book on the landscapes of Iceland and then thumbed through the vinyl collection. She settled on Erik Satie and, about ten minutes later, was quite relaxed. She was vaguely aware of Boo coming and going. She also felt the urge to text Brendon—to maybe say, *Hey, you'll never guess what I'm doing...*

But she resisted the urge, thinking of how fun it would be to tell him after the fact. She couldn't wait to see the look on his face. And with that thought, she found herself once again lingering on the idea of Brendan Peck. She did not want to go so far as to say she missed him, but...well, yeah. She missed him. But she also knew she couldn't allow herself to—

Her thoughts crashed like glass to a marble floor as Boo, out of nowhere, leaped to his feet and started unleashing a series of barks. It terrified her at first, sure, but she was also a little relieved to have been diverted from risky thoughts of Brendan.

Boo seemed to be focusing his attention on the armchair on the other side of the room. His growls and barks weren't nearly as vicious as they had been at Mrs. Grace's house, but there was still some fight in them. He edged closer to the armchair, still barking. He looked to her quickly, as if making sure she was okay, and then instantly back to the chair. Then, in a flash so quick Marie would have missed it if she blinked, Boo turned and gave chase to something. He went through the living room entrance and into the foyer, where he continued to bark.

Marie froze up a bit, once again faced with the question of what was really happening. If he was indeed chasing something, that something had been in the room with them. It had been unseen and, for all she knew, could have been staring her down the entire night.

48

In her mind, Marie envisioned someone sitting in that armchair, and Boo barking at them until they got up. Then when they *did* get up, he chased them to the foyer to make sure they were really leaving. That's exactly how the entire scene played out. Seconds later, Boo came walking back into the room. He gave the armchair a wary look before settling down.

She smiled at him and said, "Good boy."

She realized then that she was starting to feel protective of Boo. He seemed to be okay, but still...

His ear perked up at her, but only for a moment. Oddly enough, he leaped back to his feet and stared at the corner directly beside where Marie was sitting.

My God, is there something behind me?

As the question went through her head, there was a moment where she was certain this was the case. She could feel it, a presence behind her even though there was clearly no one standing there.

Again, Boo let out a series of barks and this time wasted little time running out of the room. Marie got to ger feet, curious. She watched as, just a handful of moments later, he came back into the room again...and then instantly went rushing out, barking at something else. This time, the object of his attention was farther down the hallway.

She watched Boo do this another four times in the next half an hour. She wasn't sure if it was the same presence coming back only to be chased away again or if it was a new presence each time.

After the fourth occurrence, Boo went to the front door and started scratching at it. He let out a sound of urgency, something between a growl and a whine.

"You need to go out?" she asked.

He barked, still pawing frantically at the back of the door. Marie opened it slowly and Boo went racing out instantly. He leaped down the stairs in one bound and started chasing something. If she didn't know any better, she would have thought he might be chasing after a deer or a rabbit. It was hard to see him out there in the yard even with the porch lights on. But his shape was evident enough. It took her a few moments to realize that he was running around in a circle, barking skyward at something.

Again, to someone who didn't know what was going on, the entire scene might have been comical; Boo racing around, running in circles and apparently barking at the night sky. She wasn't sure how long he did this; it was long enough for her to start worrying that Boo was going to exhaust himself.

It took another five minutes before Boo stopped barking and running in his little loop. He sniffed around the yard for a while before relieving himself against a tree and then heading back to the porch. He barely gave her a glance as he walked up the stairs and waited at the door to be let back inside. They entered the living room together, but Boo slowly made his way around the house again. Marie sat and waited, uneasy with how job-oriented Boo had become. When he had blasted outside, it had scared her—but she wasn't quite sure why. All she knew was that when he was finally done Boo came back into the living room. He leaped up onto the couch with her, settled his head on her lap, and slowly drifted off to sleep.

In the same way she could sense the job had been done at Mrs. Grace's house, she felt it in Wallace's house as well. The place seemed more peaceful, the air a little less thick. She could feel it almost at once, like someone removing a jacket from her shoulders so she could rest better.

She figured with the job over, she could return home whenever she wanted. Posey had volunteered to watch over the place again, something Marie felt incredibly guilty about. It had already been twice in one week, and the poor woman still wasn't getting paid.

But Boo was sleeping, so she did not want to bother him. After the hectic job he'd just done, the pooch deserved a rest. So Marie sat there, listening to the Satie record, while her amazingly gifted dog got some sleep.

And as he rested, she could not help but wonder what this second successful job might mean for them, and what their futures might hold.

CHAPTER TEN

When Boo woke up, Marie did not leave right away. She felt it was her responsibility to stay for a while longer, just to make sure the presence within the home was indeed gone. When Boo made one last circuit of the house at 1:45 and came back to her in a pleasant mood, Marie felt that it was okay to call it a night. She and Boo left Wallace Jackson's home at 1:55 and drove back to Port Bliss. As she neared the town and looked out to that vast, dark ocean she thought again of her mother. The night ocean, with its invisible horizon and seemingly limitless depths, was a pretty accurate representation of how her mother occupied her mind every now and then. Dark, murky, without end.

Marie rolled her eyes at the melodramatic thought. She pulled her car into the June Manor driveway at 2:11 and was asleep in bed by 2:30.

She was stirred awake at 7:40 in the morning. She saw the time on her ringing phone and felt guilty for sleeping in until such an hour. After all, she had a business to run.

She answered groggily, not even looking at the number. "June Manor, this is Marie speaking. How can I help you?"

"You did it, didn't you?" Wallace asked with cheer in his voice. "Whatever was happening here, you stopped it. I can feel it. The air is...I don't know...*cleaner*. That's not the right word, but close enough."

"So, you're back home, I take it?" Marie asked.

"Have been for about an hour. I walked the place over and it just feels different. I feel free. For the first time in a long time, I feel..."

He paused for a moment, and Marie thought he might be weeping. She gave him a moment as she finally slid out of bed and stretched a bit.

"Can I ask you something?" he asked. "Do you think it means there were actual ghosts here? Spirits, or whatever?"

"I think so," she said. "Honestly, sir, I'm still not one hundred percent sure I even believe in the traditional idea of ghosts. But yes...I

51

believe there was legitimately something there in your house and we were able to get rid of them."

She grimaced, realizing she'd said *we*. She really didn't want to explain that she'd used Boo at all—much less that he had done all of the hard work. Instead, it seemed Wallace had caught another word.

"Them?"

"Yes, sir. I believe there was more than one...*presence* in the house."

"Huh. I always thought there were a few but...tell me, Ms. Fortune. Do you think each ghost or presence, at you called it, belonged to someone that might have died in the house?"

It was something Marie had never actually thought of before. Yes, she assumed that if ghosts did in fact exist, they were the remnants of people who had passed away, perhaps trapped or otherwise lost. But she had never stopped to consider that they might be specific to a location. And now that it took root in her head, she was very much awake and wondering about June Manor. She'd seen Boo chase at least one menacing force out of the house. She wondered who it might have belonged to and if they had some sort of attachment to the house.

"I honestly couldn't say," she said. She knew her voice was distant, as most of her focus and attention was now on the mystery of it.

"Well, what do I owe you?" he said.

"I don't know that, either," she said.

They spent the next three minutes coming to terms regarding payment. She did a great job remaining professional while speaking to him, but let her elation out as she hung up the phone. She allowed herself a little fist pump, knowing that yet another eight thousand dollars would be in her bank account by the end of the day. She'd made almost thirty thousand dollars in the last two days. It wasn't a fortune, but it was more than enough to keep things afloat in terms of the bed-and-breakfast. And she hadn't had that much money in her checking account in a very long time.

When the conversation was over, Marie was very much awake. She started pacing, trying to absorb all that was happening. In her pacing, she found herself exiting her bedroom. By the time she reached the stairs and was halfway up them, she realized where she was going. It was a decision she'd made without even realizing it.

When she came to the top of the stairs, she did her best to be very quiet, not wanting to disturb her new, bizarre guest, Mr. Atticus

Winslow. Still, she could not resist stopping and cocking her head to listen. She stood there for a moment, pretty sure he was speaking inside. His voice was very low, nothing more than a droning sort of murmur. Not only could she not make out the words, but she was starting to feel like a voyeur.

She tiptoed by his closed door and went to the end of the hallway. The door at the end was closed and when she opened it, she felt an air of mystery to the place—a sensation that was only heightened when she walked to the closet.

The shoddy door to the hidden room was closed. She opened it slowly, almost as if she was discovering it for the first time. The inside was the same as it had been yesterday; the table, the book, the single chair, and the seeming lack of anything else. She stepped inside and looked at the book. She didn't sit in the chair; she felt like she'd be disturbing the place too much if she did.

The book was very old, the pages crisp and slightly yellowed. It was slightly larger than a modern hardback book. According to the header at the top of the pages, the book was called *Do the Dead Believe in Ghosts?* It seemed to consist of a hodgepodge of non-fictional ghost stories and scientific approaches on how to prove their accuracy. However, the topic of the book wasn't quite as interesting to her when she noticed a few irregularities along the stack of turned pages, already read. She went back to the beginning of the book and found several loose items tucked between the cover and the title page. Most of them were old photographs, the Polaroid kind that had to be shaken once exposed to light.

There were seven in all. Six of them featured a much younger Aunt June—easily thirty or forty years younger. In one of the pictures, there was a younger woman next to Aunt June. The woman was strikingly pretty and very pregnant. The face was unmistakable, as was the smile.

My mother…

The room suddenly felt cold as Marie tucked the pictures back into their place. She thumbed through the book for other items that had been stashed away and found several. There was a wedding invitation to people she had never heard of, dated June 26, 1972. She also found a postcard written to "June-Bug" from a man name Emil, sent from Puerto Rico; the postmark was dated August 2, 1980. There were more pictures, some of people she did not know, but most featuring Aunt June with an assortment of friends.

She felt tears coming to her eyes and wasn't quite sure why. She stepped away from the table and backed out of the room. She would come back later and spend a considerable amount of time looking at the pictures and explore any other secrets the book might have. For now, there was just too much going on inside of her head. In particular, she was still hung up on the question Wallace Jackson had asked her.

Were ghosts that haunted a property there because they had died there?

And if so, why did they hang around?

It made her wonder about June Manor, as well as Bloom Gardens and Rest and Wallace's house. As far as June Manor went, she was pretty sure there had never been any deaths in the house aside from Aunt June herself. She supposed a quick call to Deputy Miles would clear that up. As for Wallace, she had no idea. He hadn't said as much, and she didn't want to assume. She tried to recall the story Mrs. Grace had told her about a death or two in her house and decided to call her later.

She went downstairs (again quietly passing by Atticus Winslow's room) and found Posey sitting at the dining room table. She was sipping on coffee and scrolling through Facebook on her phone.

"Good morning, boss," she said.

"Hey, Posey," she said, feeling guilty. "You know, unless you really like it here, there's no need for you to be here."

"I know. But if I'm being honest with you, I'm hoping to catch a peek of this Winslow character. He seems too mysterious to me, you know?"

"*Mysterious* is a good word for it, yes."

Marie poured herself a cup of coffee and excused herself to the back porch. While she drank her coffee and looked out to the ocean, she did her best to recall if Aunt June had ever, at any point during Marie's childhood, mentioned someone dying in the house she now called June Manor—and some paranormal corners online referred to as the Ghostly Grounds.

She figured there was no sense in tormenting herself over it. She pulled out her phone and placed a call to the Winscott County Police Department. She was pretty sure the woman who answered was the same one she had spoken to when she visited Deputy Miles to ask about her mother's case. She was greeted with a very cheerful hello and asked if she needed help.

"I was hoping to speak with Deputy Miles," Marie said.

"I'm sorry, but he's out at the moment. Is this a pressing matter? If so, I can put you through to an officer."

"No thank you," she said, hanging up.

Rather than putting her phone away, she pulled up another number. It rang twice on the other end before the sweet sound of Mrs. Grace's voice answered. "Hello?"

"Hi, Mrs. Grace. This is Marie Fortune. I just wanted to check up to make sure everything was still going okay."

"Oh, absolutely. This house feels like such a new place, I'm meeting with an interior designer today to give it a makeover."

"That sounds fun! But there's one other thing I wanted to double-check. And it may sound morbid. You told me people had died in that house. A woman who killed her husband in self-defense and the original owner killed himself, right?"

"That's right."

"And you said you've been living there for eight years, right?"

"Coming up on nine, but yes...eight. Why, dear?"

"Just compiling some data," she said. It was *mostly* honest, but with a tinge of being a lie as well. "And just one more question, if you don't mind. Who was the real estate company that sold you the house?"

"I didn't go through an agency, dear. It was an independent property developer, name of Avery Decker."

Of course it was, Marie thought. She could still recall his visit to June Manor, trying to buy it away from her. To think he had worked with Mrs. Grace made her dislike the man even more. She slowly started to piece together something of a small-town conspiracy in her mind, but there was one more piece to the puzzle before she could finalize it.

She ended the call with Mrs. Grace and then called Wallace Jackson back. He apparently recognized her number because he gave her a bright and beaming "Well hey again," when he answered the phone.

"Hi, sorry to bother you," Marie said. She was still staring out to the ocean, the morning waves lazily licking the coast. "But I had a few really quick questions for you. First of all, how long have you owned that house?"

"It's going on about three years. Feels longer, though."

"And who did you buy the house from? Was it through a real estate company?"

"Sure was. A place called Coastal Gems, I believe. From what I understand, they're pretty big out your way."

"By any chance, have you had any dealings with a property developer named Avery Decker?"

There was a muffled little laugh from Wallace's end. "Yes, as a matter of fact. Pretty recently, too. Maybe five months ago? Six at most. Tried to buy the house from me and, to be honest, I almost sold. But I like the area and decided pretty quick after my divorce that I was going to live out the rest of my days here...whispering voices and all."

"And he never contacted you again?" Marie asked.

"He called a month after that first visit. I wasn't very polite in the way I told him not to call back. So he didn't. Why? I take it you've had a run-in with him, too?"

"Yes, you could say that. Tell me...did he have any idea your place was haunted?"

She hated saying the word, but felt that Wallace wouldn't mind. He'd certainly had it on his mind. She could still easily recall how out of sorts he had been when describing the voices he would sometime hear.

"You know, he *did* know...but I don't know how. He tried to use it as a pressure point. He said if word got out and I ever wanted to sell it, there would never be any buyers and I would never be able to get rid of the place."

"Huh," Marie said, growing angrier by the moment. "That sounds very familiar."

As she wrapped up her call with Wallace, her theory continued to develop, though it made no real sense. Three houses with strange histories...why was Decker so interested in them?

It felt like one of those things that was none of her business, something she should probably just ignore. But Decker was tied to the two houses she and Boo had visited to expel supernatural forces *and* he had come to her with his fat checkbook, too.

It was too solid of a link to ignore. And she knew if she didn't look into it, she might go a little mad.

She walked back into the house and went to the check-in desk. Fortunately, she had not thrown Decker's business card away when he left it with her. Instead, it was tucked away beneath the desk, in the little catch-all filled mostly with pens, paper pads, and business cards for local businesses.

She didn't even hesitate when she called the number on the card. And when he answered on the third ring, she did her best to sound delightful, masking the anger she was feeling toward the man.

"Well, hello there, Ms. Fortune," he answered.

"How'd you know it was me?"

"I was so sure you'd change your mind and call me back, I saved your number."

Oh, you terrible, arrogant son of a—

"I wouldn't say I've changed my mind, but I *would* like to talk to you. Maybe start to come to some sort of a deal. Are you free today?"

"No, unfortunately. But I *am* looking at a property not too far away from you later on. If you don't mind driving out to Amber Hills, I can chat with you there. We could even have lunch if you don't mind bringing something."

"No, I'm good. Just the talk will do," she said, again swallowing down the bitterness. What's the address?"

He gave it to her with a smug sort of satisfaction. It was clear he thought he had won—that he was going to get his way.

Marie could hardly wait to prove him wrong.

***

As Marie drove to the address Decker had given her, she thought of all the things she would say to him. Yet, as she drew closer to Amber Hills, the anger seemed to dissipate a bit. She was not growing nervous, but thoughtful. Did she really want to start a rivalry with someone like Decker? Lord only knew she had enough problems waiting for her back at June Manor.

This all ran rampant thorough her head as she finally reached Amber Hills. Just before she finished the drive to the house they were to meet in, she stopped to get gas. As she pumped, she thought she got a pretty good feel for the place. It was yet another small town, located twenty minutes away from Port Bliss, the sort of small town that took pride in being small but also tried to market itself as such. It was a seven-minute drive from the coast and did not present itself as a coastal town as much as a golf community.

After leaving the gas station, Marie passed two sprawling golf courses on her way to the address Avery Decker had given her, as well as three driving ranges. Boo sat in the passenger seat, staring out the windows as if he was saddened by the absolute waste of all that open green space to run around in.

When Marie arrived at the house, she was not at all surprised by the look of the place. Apparently, Avery Decker had a thing for strange-looking houses. While this house was not quite as gothic-looking as June Manor and not as stately as Bloom Rest and Gardens, it definitely had a strange vibe to it. There were little spires coming out of the roof, windows looking into a second floor that looked far too high. The porch had a Victorian appearance to it, but the rest of the house looked like a weird blend of modern beach and Colonial. Yet somehow, it all worked—if you didn't mind your brain hiccupping as it tried to piece it all together.

She parked behind a stylish work truck that had a decal with Avery Decker's name and phone number on the back. It was placed high up on the tailgate, making an attempt to look as dignified as vinyl lettering could be. She let Boo out of the car and could not help but smile when he pranced around a bit before stopping at one of Decker's front tires, cocking up his back right leg, and relieving himself.

"That's a good boy," Marie said.

Honestly, she had expected Decker to be sitting on the porch, waiting for her. Maybe even making a big show of how he had taken a chunk out of his day for her. But he was not on the porch, apparently still inside imagining all the ways he could remodel the house to push the selling price through the roof.

Marie and Boo walked up onto the porch and found the front door open, though an old yet somehow beautiful screen door separated the interior from the outside. She knocked and called out through the screen. "Mr. Decker?"

Boo crept up by her legs. He sniffed at the screen door, let out a little whining noise, and pawed at the door's frame.

"Mr. Decker?" she called again.

She rolled her eyes when she got no answer. The jerk was going to make her come looking for him. She opened the screen door and stepped inside, fuming as she started to look around. Oooh, she was going to tell him right off when she finally saw him! Of course, she doubted anything she had to say to him would deter him from trying to buy properties out from under people to profit for himself but at least she'd plant the seed in his big dumb head.

The interior of the house wasn't quite what she had been expecting. It had more of a typical beach house feel, though on a grander scale. The ceilings were higher, the wood was darker, there was a body on the floor, the—

She stopped, having taken only three steps into the house. She was standing in what served as a foyer—an open space between a hallway ahead of her, a small den to her right, and a larger living space to the left. A set of stairs sat to the side of the hallway, just before the larger living space, and that's where the body was lying on the floor.

CHAPTER ELEVEN

"Oh my God," Marie breathed.

Her first instinct was to run, namely because the sight of the body had scared her. But her compassionate side kicked in and she assumed there might be something she could do to help. After all, the sight of a body on the floor did not automatically mean it was a *dead* body. Perhaps this person had simply been hurt or suffered some sort of ailment.

But as she reached the body and knelt by it, she saw the blood. It had spread around the body like a halo. It was not the first dead body she'd seen—though it *was* the first dead body she had ever seen that was not in a casket.

Go call the police, she thought. *The absolute last thing you need right now is to be linked to another dead man without having any answers.*

For a moment, her arms seemed to be frozen, the muscles still too shocked by the sight of the dead body and the blood on the floor. There was fight there, sure, but also the need to help. Finally, her arms remembered their purpose and she was able to reached for her phone...only to realize it was not in her pocket. She had left it in her car, having used the GPS to get to this address. She was turning on her heel to make a run for her car. She looked down as she did this, and it was the first time her eyes had actually taken in the man's face.

She then saw that not only was the man dead, but she knew him.

It was Avery Decker. His eyes were open, staring almost up the stairs. The pool of red coming out of his head looked almost fake. Other than her own little scrapes and cuts, including a busted lip during a basketball accident at the age of fifteen, Marie had never seen this much blood. The longer she stared at it, the harder it was to look away.

She heard a shuffling noise behind her and nearly screamed. She turned and saw that it was only Boo. He had come closer to her, not quite sniffing at the floor but making a sort of low-pitched whining noise. She wondered if he knew the man was dead and was showing his doggy respects.

60

Or maybe he, too, knew just how bad this was going to look.

Slowly, and grimacing a bit, she reached down and checked his right wrist for a pulse. She was nowhere near a qualified doctor, but it took less than five seconds for her to determine that Decker was very much dead.

Marie started to tremble as she got to her feet and slowly walked backward. When Boo let out a little bark behind her, she nearly screamed.

She turned toward Boo just as she heard the noise of the screen door opening. At first, she thought the man she saw standing there was the killer. But he looked just as confused and horrified as she was. He was younger-looking, perhaps thirty at most, and was wearing a blue polo shirt was the Coastal Gems logo on the pocket.

"What...who...?" the man—a Realtor, presumably—said.

Marie could find no words and was very confused to the see that the Realtor was slowly backing away from her.

That's when she realized that he had walked in just as she was stepping away from what was clearly a very recently deceased man, with a pool of blood around his head. She knew what it must look like, but she was still so horrified by the discovery that she could not bring any words to her tongue.

"Who are you?" the man asked. He was now standing in the doorway, hovering between the need to get answers and the desire to run away from this gruesome scene.

"My name is Marie. I was supposed to meet Mr. Decker here and....he was like this when I got here."

The man looked back and forth between the corpse and Marie. "You sure he's dead?"

"Yes. There's no pulse."

"You checked?"

"Of course I checked! I came in here and he was—"

She stopped here, fully understanding what was going on. She knew how it must look and even though the idea was preposterous to her, this man did not know her at all.

She was too panicked and aghast to say much of anything at first. She watched him closely and saw that he was slowly backing out onto the front porch.

Finally, Marie managed to let out a weak, "No," but nothing else. And then, with a panicked look back to Avery Decker's body, she ran out the door and saw the real estate agent was locking himself in his car. He was on the phone, speaking animatedly to someone that Marie assumed was the police.

CHAPTER TWELVE

With the idea that the police were on their way and this could quickly become a very sticky situation, Marie started for her car, where she had left her phone. But she did not want the man who had walked in on her to think she was trying to escape. Besides, she had been the first on the scene to discover Decker's body. And because she had checked his pulse, her prints were probably on his wrist.

If she left now, it would cause more problems. So, still shaking a bit, she took a seat on the porch steps. Boo sat at her feet and let out a little whine.

The Realtor opened his door up and barely poked his head out. "I don't know who you are or what you've done," he called out. "But the police are on their way. I've been told to call them back if you try to leave."

All of a sudden, Marie felt a familiar creeping sensation. Once again, there was a dead body and she was somehow a suspect.

"Don't worry," she said half-heartedly. "I'm not going anywhere."

She sat and waited for the police to arrive, the Realtor still looking at her from the safety of his car. And although Decker was absolutely dead and not moving an inch, Marie could swear she felt him watching her from the screen door. She could not shake the feeling as she sat and waited for the police to arrive. When a patrol car did finally pull in, she hoped it would be Deputy Miles. But neither of the two men that stepped out were Deputy Miles. She did recognize the driver as Sheriff Jenkins, though. She had not spoken to the man very much but had gotten acquainted with him during the Alfred Ryker investigation several weeks ago.

The other officer looked about as young as the real estate agent who had walked in on her in such a precarious position. He followed behind Jenkins as he walked toward the porch. The real estate agent finally got out of his car and followed behind them. He kept looking at Marie as if she were a snake that might strike out at his ankle at any moment.

"Ms. Fortune, right?" Jenkins asked.

"That's right. Good to see you again, Sheriff."

"Likewise. But I have to tell you…I wish it were under different circumstances."

"Sheriff, he was dead when I got here. I think it had just happened, because the blood…it looked fresh."

"The truck in the parking lot…the name on the back says Avery Decker. Is it him? Is he the dead man inside?"

"Yes, sir."

The young officer behind him let out a small curse under his breath. Jenkins considered something for a moment and then looked down at Marie with something far too close to contempt for Marie's liking.

"We're going to go in and look the scene over," he said. "When I come out, I'm going to talk to both of you. So stay right where you are." He looked back to the real estate agent and said, "You, too, Mr. Minor."

As Jenkins and the other officer walked into the house, Mr. Minor took a few steps away from Marie. It annoyed her, but she was a little too shaken by the discovery of the body to lash out. Instead, she just said: "I didn't do it."

"No?" Minor asked. "Then why were you here?"

"I was scheduled to meet with him to talk about a property. He asked me to meet him here. How about you?"

It was clear that Minor did not believe her. He refused to answer her question, folding his arms and looking down the driveway to the little strip of two-lane beyond. It did make her wonder, though; had local Realtors started to suspect the same things that had come to her mind? Had they also started to get suspicious?

She wasn't sure how long Jenkins and his partner were inside. When they came back out, Boo raised his head, sniffed their shoes, and then resumed his pouting. It seemed the discovery of a dead body had impacted him as well.

"You were right about one thing," Jenkins said. "This just happened."

Marie nodded and noticed the younger officer rushing out to the patrol car. She assumed he would be setting things in place such as roadblocks, sending another team out to scan the crime scene, and things like that.

With Jenkins back outside, Mr. Minor came back over. Jenkins looked at both of them, trying to size them up.

"Ms. Fortune, Mr. Rick Minor says you were here first. He said when he came to the screen door and stepped inside, he saw you crouched over the body. Is that true?"

"Yes, sir, it is. And I know how that must look. But there's a very simple explanation." She went on to tell him about Decker's visit to June Manor and his rather arrogant attempt to buy the house from her. She then went into her little investigation into other properties he had shown interest in, and the call that had led her to this house.

"So you were…what?" Jenkins asked. "Coming over to give him a piece of your mind?"

"Something like that," she said, realizing at once how bad that sounded.

"And what about you, Mr. Minor? What were you coming out here for?"

"We got word that Decker was looking at this house, so I came out here to look around. I work with Coastal Gems."

"You had no idea he would be here?" Jenkins asked.

"I knew there was a chance, but no—not for certain."

"For now," Jenkins said, "it looks like someone stabbed him, right in the neck. So I'm going to need to search your cars. Both of you. And I need both of you to stay here until we get forensics out here to look the place over thoroughly."

"Yes, sir," Minor said as he gave Marie an angry scowl.

"Yes, sir," Marie echoed.

She felt herself wanting to cry. How was she in this place again? She was starting to think that maybe she had somehow cursed herself by coming to Port Bliss. Yes, she had acquired her dream of a coastal bed-and-breakfast, but at what cost? The transition had started due to Aunt June's death and ever since then, it seemed that's all her life had been: the murder of Alfred Ryker, now the apparent murder of Avery Decker…and, of course, all of the supposed ghosts.

She dwelled on this as she went to her car and sat on the hood. Boo curled up at the front, resting in the shade the car provided. Marie looked to the house as Jenkins walked back in, waiting for more police to arrive and hopefully prove, for a second time, that she was not a killer.

***

Deputy Miles arrived half an hour later, accompanied by three other men who seemed to make up the forensics team. As the three other men walked up to the house, Miles stopped by Marie's car and shook his head in a playful sort of way. But underneath it, Marie was pretty sure he seemed to be genuinely concerned.

"Seems bad luck just follows you, doesn't it?" he asked her.

"I know what this looks like," she said. "But you've got to know..."

He nodded his head and said, "Yeah, I've been filled in. Just now, coming up the driveway, though, I spoke with Sheriff Jenkins on the phone. I asked him to be the one to speak to you about news that just came across the wire."

"What news?"

"On the way up here, you stopped by the Gas 'n' Go, right? About eight or nine miles away from here?"

"Yeah. I had to fill the car up. Got some snacks, too."

"Well, Jenkins had a unit swing by there after he called for backup. I was part of that unit. I spoke to the cashier and the curious old man that seems to have sprouted roots and grown into the curb on the side of the street. Showed them your picture, then a picture of Rick Minor, the Realtor. Asked if you had stopped by or if they had seen you and the cashier said she *thought* she recognized you. Said she thought you got a bottled water and a candy bar."

"I did! They're both in my car. Well...not the candy bar. That's gone."

"I hate to say such a thing," Miles said. "But the cashier seemed like she might barely even remember her own name at times. Looked a little tired...red eyes and seepy, if you get my drift."

"Yeah, I got that impression, too," Marie said. "But she remembered me, right?

"She did. But without any accurate times, we can't get it to line up definitively. You said you filled your car up. You one of those weirdos that has the machine print out a receipt by any chance?"

"No."

"Did you get the receipt from the cashier for your purchases?"

She sighed and shook her head.

"If it comes to that, we can get that from the store...a carbon copy of it. Now, in regards to Decker, it hasn't been very long since he was killed, but it's been more than twenty-two minutes. Based on when I expect you stopped by the store—and I'm giving you a window of a few minutes here—and the time I got the call I from Sheriff Jenkins, I can't eliminate you from the realm of possibility."

"Sir, you know I didn't…"

"I believe you didn't, yes. But until we can one hundred percent take you out of the running, you *are* a suspect." She grinned, though it looked sad in nature, when he added: "You should know the rules by now, right?"

"What about him?" Marie asked, nodding up to where Minor was speaking to Sheriff Jenkins.

"We've got someone speaking to his supervisor at Coastal Gems right now, trying to work out a timeline. But for now…no, he's not quite off the chain." He looked up toward the house, hands on his hips. As he thought about what to say next, Boo came over and sniffed him. When the dog realized he had met this man before and were, by the rules and regulations of doggy etiquette, friends, he sat patiently and waited to be petted.

"I know it's old hat for you by now," Deputy Miles said, "but I need you to stick around. Don't leave Port Bliss for the next few days until we get this sorted out. Even though it looks like you're not under scrutiny, you *were* the first person to see the body. We'll probably need to talk to you again."

She nodded. "And what about now?"

"Hang out for a bit just in case forensics needs to ask you some questions." He started for the house and then, as if the thought had just come to him, he turned back and asked: "Why were you meeting him, anyway?"

She cringed and said, "I was going to ask him some questions. He came by June Manor a few days ago and tried to convince me to sell. He tried to bully me into selling my house and…it's a whole long story."

"Then I'm sure I'll end up hearing it before this case is closed."

With that, he walked up to the house. Boo looked up at Marie, looking quite sad that Miles had not petted him. But Marie was still hung up on the last thing Miles had said. Was it just her imagination, or had there been some speculation in that comment?

With a shaky hand, Marie pulled out her phone and called Posey. The cheerful cook answered after the first ring.

"Hey, Posey," Marie said. "I may need you to man the stations for a bit this evening. I'm a little tied up. Can you do that for me?"

"Oh, sweetie, I'm a little tied up myself. I'm so sorry."

"It's okay." *It's not like I'm paying you well enough to be at my call whenever I need you,* Marie thought.

"You sound distressed," Posey said. "Oh goodness, what's happened now?"

With a trembling little chuckle, she answered: "You're not going to believe this…"

CHAPTER THIRTEEN

By the time she finally got back to June Manor, the reality of it all came crashing down on Marie. For the second time, she was a murder suspect. She'd been in Port Bliss less than three months and somehow, her name was going to be associated with yet *another* murder.

She thought about what this might mean as she partially collapsed into one of the sitting room chairs upon returning home. When she realized that she would go nuts just dwelling on it, she went outside and watched as Benjamin started to work on the walkway out to the beach. Usually, she enjoyed watching the place come together but something about being outside, out in the open, made her feel exposed and uneasy. So she went back inside and started tidying up.

As she was ruthlessly dusting the stair rails, she got a text from Posey. Marie's stomach dropped when she read it.

News about that Decker creep's murder is already all over town!

Marie checked the time. It was 3:05. She'd been home for a little less than two hours. Decker had been dead for less than five. And somehow, the news was already circulating around Port Bliss. She pocketed her phone, entirely frustrated, in awe of how quickly this sort of news spread.

It was just forty minutes later when she heard the first ding on her phone—a notification from her booking app. She tried not to link the murder with the email she read, showing that a future guest had cancelled their reservation.

This was not as easy to do as the day wound on. She got another of those dings just before bed. Another cancellation, this one from a guest who had been due to arrive in just five days.

And then the social media comments started coming in. She received four Facebook comments by midnight, both from people she had never met. They were meant to be good-natured, she supposed, but they creeped her out.

One of them asked: *Dude, are you trying to start a campaign for opening some sort of real-life murder mystery situation at your B and B?*

The other stated: *It's sort of cheating if you're killing people to make more ghosts to go chasing after…*

She hated that social media was such a double-edged sword. She knew it was a necessity to run a business these days, but she hated that it also left June Manor (and herself) so vulnerable and exposed. She was in the sitting room—a strangely peaceful place late at night—reading some tips and tricks online on how to better filter out these sorts of comments when her cell phone rang. She was afraid some might have gone so far as to call her with those kinds of messages, but she let out a sigh of relief when she saw Brendan Peck's name on the caller display.

She answered it, trying to think of something witty and clever to say. But she had nothing, so she settled with a simple "Hey."

"Hey," Brendan said. "Sorry I'm calling so late. But I just saw the news. Are you okay?"

"Been better," she said. "And how did you see the news? This happened in a small Maine town. Why am I getting emails from complete strangers teasing me about it?"

"That might be my fault," he said. "The paranormal crowd…they sort of linger. They're loyal to a fault. Some of them still talk about the original footage from your house, even if I did manage to debunk it. The fact that you will forever be linked to Alfred Ryker's death also makes you sort of a C-list staple in recent conversation in the paranormal community."

"See, you didn't tell me any of this when you first came to me with that footage," she said with a nervous laugh.

"In my defense, there's no way I could have known how things would turn out. Anyway…back to my original question. Really…*how are you?*"

"I don't even know. I've been asked to not leave Port Bliss yet again."

"Surely they don't think you're a suspect?"

She assured him that she was pretty much cleared, though not completely, walking him through all the details Deputy Miles had shared with her in regards to her visit to the Gas 'n' Go.

"I wish there was something I could do," Brendan said.

"There is: don't cancel your reservation. I've already had a couple fall through. I can't say it's for sure because of the recent news, but the timing can't be ignored."

"Nope. No cancelling for me. I'm actually looking forward to swinging by there again."

He left a silent beat after the comment, as if giving her the chance to question him on it. But even if she had been up to any sort of flirtatious dialogue, she still wasn't quite sure how to approach a man like Brendan Peck. So she let the opportunity slide by and carried on the conversation.

They chitchatted about more conferences he was attending, while she told him about Posey taking on more responsibilities and working on new dishes. It was all mundane and sort of boring, but when she ended the call, she did feel a bit better.

Yet as she stood up from her chair in the sitting room, she caught the briefest glimpse of someone standing in the doorway of the sitting room. When she turned to look, she was pretty sure she saw Atticus Winslow standing here, dressed in all black as always. But if he *had* been there, he had hurried away when she'd first spied him. She nearly went chasing after him, but decided not to. The man had asked for nothing but privacy and that, Marie figured, was the one thing she could give him without much trouble.

Still, she had to suppress a shiver as she thought of him, standing silently and watching her while she spoke on the phone. She slowly walked to the archway between the sitting room and the foyer, looking up the stairs. If it *had* been him looking, he'd made his way back up the stairs quietly.

What's he doing up there all alone, anyway? she wondered.

When her phone dinged at her, she jumped a bit. Turning away from the stairs and walking back into the sitting room, she checked her phone. The ding had come from the app that handled her reservations. She opened up the alert, hoping for a reservation coming in the near future.

Instead, it was another cancellation. This one was from a woman in Boston, scheduled to stay in two weeks. She had even added a message with her cancellation. It was a short one, getting right to the point. *Shame on you, killer.*

It almost made her want to cry. She collapsed back into the chair her great-aunt had once enjoyed, and wondered how much worse things could possibly get.

She realized as she sat there that the police, while very professional and well-meaning, weren't exactly known for their speed. Without any solid leads at the start of a case, she knew that it could take a while for anything of substance to come to light. And while she was fine with that in regards to having her name cleared, it was quite a different thing for someone who ran a business. If her *name* was being dragged through the mud, so was her *business.* Her two very recent cancellations was proof of this.

And while she was far from having the guile and insights of a police officer, Marie *had* already gotten a picture of how they operated. She'd had a front row seat to it while she'd been entangled in the Alfred Ryker murder. To get to the bottom of this case, they would question Avery Decker's friends, families, and co-workers. They might even question some people who knew *her* well, as well as those who knew Rick Minor well—family, friends, and all that.

All of that was fine and good and, in the end, would likely turn up results. But there was another avenue that had grabbed Marie's interest from the start. It was the same avenue she had been pursuing when she had decided to call Decker and meet with him.

What was it about these houses that had attracted Decker? And had he been harassing and bullying people in the same way he'd tried bullying her? In the very same way he had come to Wallace Jackson, looking to buy his property?

It seemed obvious to Marie that the killer would be someone whom Decker and attempted to strongarm in the past. Sure, Marie knew nothing about the man's past, but that was the great thing about living in a small town: there was always someone wanting to talk.

It just so happened, she knew exactly who to go to.

CHAPTER FOURTEEN

Going to Posey seemed like a no-brainer. The woman seemed to know everyone not only in Port Bliss but all of Winscott County. Posey arrived for the dinner shift (though there were no guests to speak of) right on time. She arrived just as Marie was doing some basic Google research, looking up the address of the house Avery Decker had been murdered in.

With a little digging, she was able to find a real estate listing for the property. This included the name of the last person to have lived in the house. The name on the title was Margaret Hampstead and, according to the listing, she had either lived in it or had it otherwise occupied it until earlier this year.

She also saw that Coastal Gems Realty had represented Mrs. Hampstead when she had purchased it. Beyond that, there was very little information to go on.

As a last-ditch effort, she ran a Google Search for *Amber Hills, Maine haunted.* The only results that came up were a few different listings for the Amber Hills Haunted Hay Ride that had taken place every October over the past several years.

Disappointed in her search results, Marie nearly called Brendan to see if he knew of any haunted areas in the Amber Hills area. She decided not to because she figured anything local that might be haunted would have already come up in conversation with him, given the way their very strange friendship was going.

"Something wrong?"

Posey's voice frightened her more than it should have. Truth be told, ever since she and Benjamin had uncovered the secret room in the upstairs hallway, most sudden noises or voices tended to make her jump more than usual. It also did not help that she was currently harboring a guest like Atticus Winslow.

But now that Posey had interjected, it gave Marie ample opportunity to hit her up for some gossip. Only...if it was useful and helpful, could it be considered gossip? Marie didn't know.

"Nothing, really," Marie answered. "Just trying to play detective."

"Ooh, on what?"

"Well, I don't suppose you know much about Amber Hills, do you?"

"Not really. I had a boyfriend that lived around there for a bit. Lots of golfing, right? Nice houses, sort of quiet. Close enough to the beach to be beach-like but far enough away to miss the sound of the waves."

"Ever hear any spooky stories from around there?"

"None that I know of. But you know, there *are* some pretty cool Civil War stories about the place."

"Really? Like what?"

Posey gave a shrug. "To be honest, history sort of bores me. I only know it because any time the Civil War is mentioned, Maine doesn't really come to mind. As far as I know, there were no actual battles fought on Maine soil. But you know...I hate to throw someone under the bus, but if you want details on Amber Hills or any of the other nearby small towns, I can point you in the right direction."

"I figured you might be able to."

"I do what I can. Anyway...have you been to On Second Thought Collectibles yet? Have you had the pleasure of meeting Mrs. Clark?"

Marie smiled. She's nearly forgotten about the kind old woman who ran Port Bliss's oldest antiques store—a store Marie had visited several times during her childhood visits to the town.

"I have! Posey, you're a saint!"

"Remember that when you open your private investigator business."

Due to the time, Marie figured it would be a safe bet to call On Second Thought Collectibles first. As she suspected, it closed at five on the dot, meaning she'd have to wait through the night to get her answers.

Which was fine, really. As per Deputy Miles's instructions, it wasn't like she was going anywhere.

***

The smell of On Second Thought Collectibles once again brought memories of her childhood rushing back. Yes, she had been inside the store twice since first arriving to Port Bliss—once on her fist stroll through town and again when looking for two additional chairs for the dining room table. But it was the sort of smell that triggered memories right away, the same way that the faint smell of glue would forever remind her of her kindergarten teacher, Mrs. Jolly.

Marie found Mrs. Clark at the back of the store, dusting off what looked to be a decanter for whiskey. When she looked up and spotted Marie, she flashed a smile. Marie took this as a good thing. Apparently, news of her appearance at a murder scene had not yet made its way to this shop…yet.

"Good to see you, Marie," she said. She then looked down at Boo and scratched him between his ears. "And you, too, Boo. Anything I can do for you today or do I get the honor of just a random visit?"

"Some of both, actually," Marie said. "Posey was telling me that you might be a good source of information about the town of Amber Hills. I was looking for some spooky stories you may have heard of."

Mrs. Clark grinned and stopped dusting. She gave Marie a very playful disappointed look. "I heard about you and that ghost hunting friend of yours. And, of course, about all the things that might be happening at June Manor. Some are calling it the Ghostly Grounds now, did you know that?"

"Yes ma'am, I'd heard."

"I take it you sort of got hooked on the ghost stories of it all?"

"In a way," she said, figuring she wasn't being totally dishonest.

"Well, I hate to disappoint you, but I don't have any ghost stories about Amber Hills. I know the area so well because my grandparents lived there. It's a cute place—or, rather, it *was* before all those damned golf courses popped up. But it does have a bloody history. Most don't know about it or, if they do, they choose to ignore it."

"Stories from the Civil War?"

"Some, yes," Mrs. Clark said. "Now, as far as I know, the only real battle to occur on Maine soil was the Battle of Portland Harbor. But there have always been rumors of a Union soldier that lost his mind. Legend has it that he simply woke up one night and started killing his fellow soldiers. He ran off and there was this terrible shootout. Depending on who tells you the story, that poor soldier committed suicide. There are actual records you can see in the local library, handwritten by the captain of his unit, stating that the soldier was screaming about hearing voices in his head just before he shot himself."

"That's terrible."

"Well, you can see why it's the sort of thing left out of historic tales of the area, right?"

75

"For sure. But there's a certain house I'm looking for, previously owned by a woman with the last name of Hampstead."

"Huh. You don't say."

"I do say. Why? Do you know of it?"

"I know where it us, yes. Not so much because of the house but because of the property it's on, though. There's a field somewhere out there in Amber Hills that is popular with deer hunters in the winter." She chuckled nervously and added: "It just also happens to have rumors around it...rumors that say hunters swear the place gives them the willies. I'm pretty sure that's the place. I know this for a fact because my husband, God rest his soul, was an avid deer and turkey hunter. He said the few times he'd been by that field, he'd get the sweats. Felt like there was someone watching him. That sort of thing. I remember him telling me one time that he felt bad for the poor family that lived in the house in front of that field, just off to the side."

"And you're sure it's the right house? On Larter Road?"

"Yeah, almost positive."

It was eerie to consider it. But, at the same time, she thought of Wallace Jackson, telling her about the voices he would sometimes hear. She wondered if they'd sounded similar to the voices the troubled Union soldier had heard.

"Now, I've never been by there," Mrs. Clark said. "No way I'd willingly go driving by a place that scared my husband. That man had guts of steel. But I recall him telling me it's a strange place—a weird house. Looks like a bunch of different building styles just tossed together."

Yep, that's the house, all right, Marie thought.

"Do you know if anyone has lived there recently?" she asked.

"Sorry, but no." Mrs. Clark paused, thought for a moment, and then looked at Marie curiously. "You're not asking me all this just for you and your ghost-hunting friend, are you?"

"No," Marie said. Mrs. Clark had all but confirmed that the house Avery Decker had been killed in was the house in front of this supposedly cursed field. "It's something else, actually."

"Well, I hope what I told you was good for something other than a scare. Are you okay, dear? You do look a bit flustered."

"I'm fine," Marie said. But really, even as she and Boo gave their goodbyes and exited the store, she thought about sitting in the car in front of the house in Amber Hills and wondered what sorts of things might have been watching her.

And, beyond that, she wondered just how much of the property's history Avery Decker had known before he'd been killed.

Perhaps even more importantly, what might he have known that would cause someone to kill him?

It seemed like a dangerous question, one that would make most sensible people turn away and run. But Marie figured she had thrown *sensible* out the window the first time she saw footage of her dog chasing ghosts away.

With hidden rooms, haunted houses, and people being killed left and right, her life in Port Bliss was apparently not going to be a sensible one. Not unless she could find some answers that would hopefully lead her to once again clearing her name.

CHAPTER FIFTEEN

After leaving Mrs. Clark's shop, she went back to the bed-and-breakfast, got in her car, and drove back to Wallace Jackson's house. Marie was usually not the type to just drop by someone's house unannounced, but she had so many ideas and thoughts circling around in her head that good manners were the least of her concern. She thought she might know where to start her impromptu investigation but, as always, had no idea what questions to ask. She was far from a detective or even a novice sleuth, but figured the best place to start would be with others who had endured run-ins with Avery Decker.

While it was *technically* considered leaving the town limits of Port Bliss, she didn't think she'd be breaking any laws, so long as she remained in Winscott County.

When she arrived at the house, she wasn't all that surprised to notice that it looked different in the light of day—and in knowing she was not coming to banish spirits. The fact that Wallace was mowing his grass when she arrived also made it seem much more normal. He was driving around the side yard on a large riding lawn mower. Dressed in a T-shirt, gold shorts, and a wide-brimmed Panama Jack–style hat, Wallace himself helped to make the house look even more unthreatening.

He spotted Marie as she got out of the car, giving her a wave. He disengaged the blade and rolled the mower over to the edge of the driveway. He seemed pleased to see her, but a little confused as well.

"Hey there, Ms. Fortune," he said. "I didn't think you'd ever come back here. Did you miss the place that much?"

"Well, that's not why I'm here..."

"Ah, is it the money? Well, a transfer that big, the bank makes me wait a day or so before it will send it."

"No, it's not that, either. I had a question about your interactions with Avery Decker."

"Oh boy," Wallace said. He took his hat off, wiped some sweat away, and shrugged. "Not much to say, really. He's a piece of work, that's for sure."

"You said he only bugged you about buying your home twice, right?"

"Yeah, just that first time when he came by, visiting unannounced, and then the phone call a few weeks later. Now, truth be told, I might have deserved that phone call. See, when he came by with that first offer, it was really tempting. It would have been enough to buy some small place down in Florida and live comfortable for a few years. But in the end, I told him no. There was just something about him I didn't like."

"I didn't like him at first sight, either," Marie admitted. "And apparently, we aren't the only ones. Someone killed him yesterday."

The look of shock on his face was genuine. She watched the play of emotion, from surprise to something that looked almost like sadness. "Oh my goodness. Any idea who?"

"None. But to make things a little stickier, I was the one that found the body."

"How?" he asked, clearly surprised. He also looked a little spooked, a look Marie had quickly gotten accustomed to. "Where?"

"Another house he was trying to buy. I think I might have figured out something about him…that he's been doing his best to buy houses with strange and maybe even violent histories. I think he may have been trying to buy them at a deal, flip them, then sell them at a higher cost. Nothing wrong with that, of course…but it was the way he went about it."

"He was sort of a bully, that's for sure. And he's *dead?*"

"He is. And because I was the one that found the body—was seen *bending over* the body by a Realtor, in fact—well, that doesn't look good. So I was really just wondering if you knew anything else about Decker. Did you know of him before he came knocking at your door looking to buy the place?"

"No, but I'd heard of him. He used to work for Coastal Gems, I think. But he somehow got wrapped up in land development. Way I hear it, he was hired to design a small housing division in Ogunquit. Then he came back out this way and started buying up land and houses in Winscott County."

"Do you know of anyone else Decker tried to buy from?"

"Just one. She was a young lady, probably no more than thirty-five or so. She lived on that stretch of road between Port Bliss and Amber

Hills, back in a wooden lot. I only know about this because of the offer he gave her. Low-balled her, but she was anxious to move."

"Any idea why?"

"Sorry, I don't. Now, take all of this with a grain of salt. You know how gossip can be in small towns. I do everything I can to steer clear of it but sometimes it falls right in your lap."

"I don't guess you know the address of that property, do you?"

"No. But I think you can see it from the road. After Decker got his hands on it, he turned it into this massive coastal cottage. Rental properties, I think." He chuckled to himself and shook his head. "That man was making crazy money with all of his remodels and transformations. I hate to speak ill of the dead, but it really doesn't surprise me that someone might have been angry with him. Making that much money, dealing with lands and homes…you're bound to cross someone that holds on to grudges, you know?"

Marie considered this for a while but it was just as she had assumed: there were no real answers to be had unless she went digging in places she probably shouldn't. But even then, as she was starting to face such a defeat, another idea occurred to her. As it started to shape up and show its edges, Wallace spoke up.

"Seems you're trying to play detective, is that a safe assumption?"

"I think *detective* is too strong of a term, but something like that."

"Well, you know, if I was looking for information on someone like Decker and the properties he's built or dealt with, I'd personally start looking at the Winscott County property records, over at the county recorder's office. I mean…if it were *me*."

He gave her a wink and then cranked the mower back to life. Marie stood there a moment longer, letting the idea sink in. By the time Wallace had started on his next strip of grass, the mower puttering along, Marie was back in her car and chasing down her next idea.

CHAPTER SIXTEEN

Wallace had been right. It was easy to spot the newer and flashy property along the side of the road on Highway 33, which ran between Amber Hills and Port Bliss. It was a beautiful spot, but was sorely out of place among the other, much older and *much* simpler homes. She turned off the highway and drove down to the property. She could see no office of any kind, so she assumed the rentals were run by Decker— or, rather, *had* been.

She took a picture of the property and tagged the location on her phone's map application, and headed back for Port Bliss. With a twenty-minute drive ahead of her, she supposed it was a good opportunity to explore the next idea she had come up with.

She pulled up Brendan's number on her phone, put it on speaker, and set it on the console. Brendan answered on the second ring, his voice filling her car and making her feel a little too happy.

"Hey there," he said. "On the run from the law?"

"You're not even remotely funny," she said.

"I know. Sorry. How are you?"

"Okay, all things considered. But I find myself once again trying to clear my name. I'm trying to learn more about Avery Decker, trying to figure out who he might have wronged or majorly pissed off. And I think you *might* be able to help me."

"Okay. What can I do?"

"Well, like last time, I've been asked to not leave Port Bliss for a while. But some of the digging I'm doing turned up a potential property somewhere in Ogunquit. I was wondering if you might be willing to make a stop by there when you travel down here."

"Ogunquit is sort of out of my way coming to Port Bliss," he said.

"It might be worth your while. I'm starting to learn that Avery Decker had a thing about buying stigmatized properties and turning them for a profit."

"Stigmatized how?"

"Haunted. And these aren't just campfire stories. These are property owners that made legitimate complaints about strange things occurring in their homes. And here's the real bait for you: we're not talking about just a house in Ogunquit; it's an entire housing division."

"That *is* some enticing bait. You got an address?"

"Not yet. That's my next bit of digging. I need to find some addresses and property records."

"That sounds terribly boring," Brendan said. "But if you can find me that address, then I'll absolutely go check it out. Sounds promising."

"Thanks. I'll see you in…what is it now? Two weeks?"

"Looking forward to it."

They ended the call and Marie continued on her way to the county recorder's office. Without the GPS on her phone, she would have never found it. The building was a simple one-story structure, tucked in beside the municipal building and the library. It was pushed back behind the properties, as if its appearance needed to live up to its rather non-exciting name.

Inside, there was a counter along the back wall. The walls were a drab gray. No pictures, no decorations. A plain-looking woman peered up at her from behind the counter. From the looks of it, she had been absorbed in a book, which she slid away as Marie approached the counter.

"Can I help you?" the lady asked.

"I'm not quite sure how this works," Marie admitted. "I'm looking for the sale and development history of a few properties." This was only partly true, but she thought it sounded better than *I'm looking for information on a certain builder that just so happens to have been recently murdered.*

"Well, we've got fourteen filing cabinets in the back if you need copies of something physical. But if you're just sort of browsing, you can use one of the computers to check our database." She pointed to the far corner of the room to where two ancient-looking desktop monitors sat on a desk.

"Thanks," Marie said, finding it a little hard to believe that access to that sort of information was so readily available.

However, when she sat down behind one of the computers, it did not take her long to figure out that it wasn't going to be quite so easy. There was no real order to the way the database was laid out and, unlike basic file folder functions, there weren't many areas where she could simply click on a name or address and be taken somewhere else within the database.

She started out by putting in the address to the rentals she had snapped a picture of on the way over. She was able to see the names of the two women who managed the properties and then the owner—who was listed as Avery Decker. A little more digging also showed her the names of the construction company and developer. The developer was also listed as Avery Decker.

From there, she spent about half an hour looking for other properties Decker had had his hands in. The data went all the way back to when Decker had been working with Coastal Gems and all of those properties were rather nondescript. She could not find information so precise as to the window of time that had passed between his time with Coastal Gems and when he had gone solo, but there did indeed seem to be a unique difference in the "gems" he'd dealt in with Coastal Gems and those he pursued as a property developer.

The one good thing she had going for her was that the list of properties Decker had acquired, developed, and sold within Winscott County wasn't very long. There were seven in all, one of which was indeed Mrs. Grace's property. She kept looking, but as she had expected, there were no listings in the database outside of Winscott County.

She printed out the information on the seven local properties, which included physical addresses, current owners, and history of sale and resell over the past fifteen years. She gave the woman at the counter a wave and a word of thanks; this time, the woman didn't even bother looking up from her book.

In her car, Marie looked at the list of properties Decker had been associated with. With only seven to choose from, she figured the chances of speaking to all of the current residents might not be so hard.

Best of all, there was one address listed in Port Bliss—a house that was less than two miles away from where she was currently parked.

But before she headed over there, she figured she should go back to June Manor to pick up Boo.

Just in case.

**

The property records did not give a phone number for the owners of the property. All Marie knew was that it was owned by Richard and Karen Hudson, purchased after Decker had remodeled the home four years ago. She pulled into the Hudsons' driveway five minutes later. Two blocks away from the beach, it was a stately-looking home that eschewed the common house-on-the-beach tropes.

She was relieved to see a car in the driveway, indicating that someone was in fact home at 2:30 on a weekday afternoon. As she walked up the porch stairs, Boo trailing at her side, she tried to think of how to best introduce herself. Why was she here? Should she just skip formalities and get straight to the point? If she'd learned anything over the past few months it was that those who believed they were experiencing authentic supernatural phenomenon were usually pretty forthcoming about sharing their stories.

She figured she'd just wing it based on the Hudsons' response to an unexpected visitor. She knocked on the door, looking down at Boo for encouragement. He glanced back up, wagging his tail lazily.

A few seconds later, the door was opened by a middle-aged woman dressed in a tank top and athletic shorts. The tank top had little splatters of paint on it, and the woman held a small paintbrush in her hand.

"Yes, can I help you?" she asked.

"Are you by any chance Karen Hudson?" Marie asked.

"I am. Who might you be?" There was no real accusation to the question, but a friendly sort of curiosity.

"My name is Marie Fortune. I moved to town a little less than three months ago. I run a bed-and-breakfast in the house my great-aunt used to own."

"You mean June, right?"

"I do. Did you know her?"

"A bit. I'd run into her here and there at some of the community art shows. She played her ukulele for fun, and I tried peddling some of my paintings. I didn't know her well, but well enough to know she was a sweetheart."

"Thanks for that."

"Anyway...can I do something for you?"

"Well, I had a few questions about your house, and maybe some of the story about how you came to buy it."

"Can I ask why?"

"I'm looking into the man I think might have sold you the house. A guy named Avery Decker."

"Oh yeah. I remember him well. He was…well, he was a whole lot." She tapped the thin end of her paintbrush against her chin, thinking for a moment. "Come on in," she said. "And your furball can come in, too."

Karen led them through the house's central hallway. The house was a gorgeous classic sort of home, somewhere between a Colonial and old farmhouse build. Marie had no real time to look things over, as Karen led them quickly toward the back of the house. She guided them into a large sunroom that overlooked a back yard that was covered in flowers. The sunroom was apparently used as a miniature painting studio. There were canvases with several different subjects: a very zoomed in perspective of a lily, a gull on a fence post, a nude woman sitting on sand, and an incomplete one of what looked like it was going to be a man fishing from a pier.

"These are incredible," Marie said. She wasn't just being kind. The lily in particular was stunning.

"Thanks! That one," she said, playfully sneering at the painting of the lily, "just about drove me insane. Anyway…Avery Decker. What do you need to know?"

Karen placed her paintbrush into a small jar filled with a few other brushes and dirty water. Boo was slowly circling the room, sniffing at the bottoms of the stands containing canvases. Apparently, he smelled something a little too strong for his nose, as he sneezed a few times before backing away.

"Well, I suppose I should go ahead and tell you now before you hear about it *after* I've left and the whole thing just seems even weirder…but Decker was found dead yesterday. Looks like he was murdered in a house he was looking to redevelop and sell."

"Oh my God. That's terrible."

Marie was pretty sure Karen meant it. She cupped a hand smeared with navy-colored paint to her mouth in shock. Her eyes darted left to right, clearly confused and horrified as she took in the information.

"Murdered?" she asked, as if she did not understand the word.

"Yes."

"That's just terrible."

"I agree. However, not long before he was killed, he and I had an awkward meeting. He rolled right up to my house and almost demanded to buy it—not caring that it had once belonged to my great-aunt and that I am currently trying to run a bed-and-breakfast out of it."

"Yeah, that sounds about right," Karen said. "Don't get me wrong, he was just as accommodating as he could be when he helped my husband and me pick out this house. But he *does* have a strong personality. Er...*did* have a strong personality, I suppose."

"Well, I asked around to see if he had made other brash attempts at buying properties, and I did find a few. More than that, I found something of a link between them. And I was wondering if your home may also be linked to a discovery I made..."

"What sort of link?" Karen asked. The tone in her voice indicated that she just *knew* something bad was about to be brought to light.

"Well, it's going to sound absolutely nuts, but I was wondering if you had ever experienced anything out of the ordinary during your time here."

Karen started nodding knowingly at once. She crossed her arms over her chest and said: "You mean the ghosts?"

The question caught Marie off guard and for a moment, she had no idea what to say. Slightly dumbfounded, she could only nod. *Why is this sort of thing starting to feel all too normal to me?* she wondered.

"Yeah, it's annoying," Karen said. "We were pretty sure there was something strange about this house three days after we had fully moved in. It took about two months before my husband and I started actually referring to it as ghosts."

"And you've been here for four years, right?"

"Give or take a few months, yes."

"Would you mind telling me what sorts of things you've experienced?"

Karen sighed and sat down on the little couch. It, like her clothes, was splattered with paint. "It's strange because when you say 'ghost,' you expect this horrific story. But for us, nothing really scary has happened. Things will move here and there and on occasion, you think you've seen something or someone standing right beside you, but when you turn to face them they're gone. The only thing I can think of that is actually *frightening* are the few instances where we wake up in the middle of the night. For a minute, you can swear there was someone there at the foot of the bed, talking. And while you can't see anyone or anything, you feel a presence in the room. And it's not a very friendly one. It's sort of like…like a *pressing*. Like someone is not happy you're there."

Marie had to suppress a little chill. She opened her mouth to ask another question but was interrupted by a familiar yet unexpected sound. Somewhere else within the house, Boo was barking. Marie looked around the sunroom, confused. She hadn't even noticed Boo had left.

"Oh my gosh, I'm so sorry," Marie said. "He sometimes has—"

When his barks became growls, Marie's heart stuttered in her chest. She looked at Karen and saw the woman giving her a concerned look. "What the hell is he doing?" she asked.

Playing fetch, I think, she thought. *Just not with balls or sticks.*

"I'm so sorry," Marie said. "I'll get him…"

She went racing out of the sunroom, calling for him. "Boo! Come here, boy!"

The growls and barking were coming from the front of the house. As she approached the kitchen, she came to a skidding halt as Boo came running into the hall. He had been in the kitchen, apparently chasing something around the sizeable island in there.

Marie watched him with concern and, for just a moment, thought she saw something in front of him—something running. It was barely there at all, so slight she was sure she was imagining it.

"Do you…did you see that?" she asked Karen.

"See what?"

Great, you're seeing things now, Marie thought. *You're so involved in this madness that you're forcing yourself to see things.*

"I don't know," Marie said. "Probably nothing."

Boo made it to the front door and then stopped. When he stopped running, he also stopped barking and growling. He stared at the front door for a moment and then turned in a little half-circle until he faced Marie and Karen Hudson. He looked a little unsure of himself, like a dog that wasn't sure if he was about to get scolded by his master.

"Does he do that often?" Karen asked. Her voice was soft, wavering, and slightly afraid.

"You know, I'd really like to say no…but it wouldn't be the total truth."

The two women stood in silence for a moment, looking at Boo. For Marie, it was a moment that struck her as profound for no reason at all.

It was simply the feeling and knowledge that she was getting extremely attached to a dog she had never asked for or really even wanted.

"You know," Karen said, "I don't know what the appropriate etiquette is for something like this. Do I invite you stay for a cup of tea, or do I ask you to leave my house as quickly as you can?"

"Maybe somewhere in between," Marie said. "How about I thank you for your information on the house and then give a polite goodbye?"

Karen grinned nervously and nodded her head. "Yes. Sounds good. I'd say it was nice to have met you…but truth be told, it was a little weird."

Still, Karen remained polite as she walked with Marie to the front door. Marie noticed that she was looking around slowly, as if making sure the thing Marie claimed she saw wasn't lurking around a corner. She gave Marie a little wave as she and Boo headed down the porch stairs, and then closed the door.

When Marie and Boo were back in the car, Marie looked at him and cupped his face. Placing his nose to hers, she said: "I'm not sure you understand how this works, but I have to be in charge of our little operation. You may have just cost me a job."

She meant it as a joke but felt the truth to it. That was three times now—three different times Boo had gone crazy, apparently chasing something supernatural out of a house. Actually, it was four times if she counted his first time in June Manor.

As she drove back home, she glanced to Boo as he looked out the window. She reached out and stroked his back, realizing how special he really was. In terms of parting gifts from deceased relatives, Boo was sort of perfect.

And given Aunt June's oddball personality, Marie couldn't help but wonder if there was much more for her to learn from Boo and, in tandem, June as well.

CHAPTER SEVENTEEN

"Our buddy Boo looks tired," Posey said as she sat down at the dining room table. She had just placed a taco bake on the table; Marie was dumbfounded by how the woman could make something as simple as a taco bake seem like a gourmet meal.

"Yeah, we had a busy day," Marie said as she served herself.

It was clear that Posey was thinking of asking about this, but decided not to. She gave Boo, who was lying in the entryway between the sitting room and dining room, a final glance before filling her plate.

Dinner once again consisted of Marie and Posey sitting alone. While she *technically* had a guest, it was hard to view Atticus Winslow as such. He remained confined to his room and she had not heard a peep out of him since he'd checked in. There had been the one instance where she thought she'd caught him eavesdropping on her conversation, but that was about it.

"You hear from Mr. Winslow at all today?" Marie asked as they ate. Tonight's dinner was delicious. It was a shame she was the only one getting to enjoy Posey's gift.

"Not a word," Posey said. "Although, if you give me permission to do so, I think I could probably lure him out with food."

"Use all the smells and cooking trickery you want," Marie said. "But he's asked that we not physically disturb him, so I'm going to observe that wish. Also…you know, Posey, you've basically become an assistant as well as a cook. I'd like to start paying you. For right now, I can't guarantee a routine schedule but at least I can offer *something.*"

"You don't need to do that, sweetie."

"You keep saying that, but at some point, I have to stop taking advantage of your kindness. As a matter of fact, I'd like to write you a check in a few days."

"I won't keep refusing if you keep insisting," Posey said with a smile. "Would this sudden financial generosity have anything to do with your recent side gig?"

"Maybe." She smiled right back as she said it, leaving it at that. While Posey was more or less her only real friend in town and knew the basics about what she and Boo did when they left together, she didn't want to overwhelm the woman and potentially scare her away.

The ladies cleaned up from dinner, and Posey called it a night. Marie made a note to write her a check—somewhere in the neighborhood of two thousand dollars, though she'd nearly made it for more. The woman had cooked countless breakfast and dinners, and had spent the past week or so acting as an assistant, always stepping up and being present at the manor while Marie was out and about chasing off ghosts with Boo or digging up dirt on Avery Decker.

When Posey was gone, Marie looked up the stairs. She did not *go* upstairs, but looked up to the top floor, thinking. She wanted to go back into that hidden room. She wanted to look at the pictures and the book and try to figure out what kind of secrets Aunt June might have been hiding in there.

But honestly, the mere thought of it was exhausting. The last two days had piled a ton of stress and information. There was the discovery of Decker's body, her being eyed as a suspect, revelations about Decker's shady work history, Boo's unexpected and unscheduled ghost run at Karen Hudson's house, and the overall creepiness of the single guest she was currently boarding.

If she went to the secret room and uncovered anything else, she feared her brain might literally start melting.

So instead of going upstairs, Marie retired to the one place that used to bring her the most peace and relaxation; she walked out to the back porch to watch the ocean. She leaned against the deck rail and watched the white caps break out of the seemingly abysmal darkness of the night sea. It was hypnotic—even more so when she closed her eyes, breathed in, and just listened to the crashing of the waves. In these moments, she could easily imagine Aunt June standing on this same spot, enjoying the same sights and sounds. She also wondered if her mother had stood here in this same spot at some point Maybe she had; maybe the pregnant version of her mother she'd seen in the pictures in the secret room had stood right here, Marie growing inside of her, starting that mother-daughter connection with Port Bliss and the ocean.

And just like that, the secret room was back in her thoughts. She wondered if June had always expected her to find it. When she'd had the last-minute change of heart and placed Marie in her will to own the house, had she assumed her great-niece would one day find that room?

While her time on the deck had indeed helped to clear her mind and calm her nerves, Marie found herself heading back inside, toward the stairs. There was, after all, *a hidden room* in the house her great-aunt had given her. She figured it was natural to remain constantly curious about such a thing.

She started up the stairs slowly, being as quiet as she could. She told herself it was so she would not disturb Mr. Winslow, but the truth of the matter was that she was hoping to hear something from the other side of his door. Music, his end of a phone conversation—anything that might clue her in to what he might be up to.

She was halfway up the stairs when someone knocked on the front door. Marie was engaged in her clumsy stealth mode when the noise reached her ears and she just about jumped in the air and screamed. Instead, she gasped, held her breath, and felt her heart jackhammering in her chest.

It was nearly 10:30 at night, so she had no clue who could be knocking. Her positive side told her it might be some tired weary traveler looking for last-minute lodging. Yet, in a small town like Port Bliss, she knew this was not likely the case. So as she went back down the stairs, it was literally like playing a guessing game. *Who's the guest behind Door Number One?*

When she answered the door, she grinned widely. If she *had* been playing a guessing game, she would have lost.

Brendan Peck stood on the porch, grinning right back at her. "I know it's late and I should have probably called first…but where's the fun in that?"

"No, it's okay. I'm glad you're here." She was doing her best to tamp down her level of excitement but wasn't sure she was doing a very good job. In fact, it was taking everything in her power not to hug him.

"Got any rooms available?"

"Oh, I don't think so. But I can move some people around."

As she led him inside, Boo came rushing to them. He ran a few circles around Brendan's feet, clearly remembering him. Brendan hunkered down and petted the dog, tousling his ears and rubbing his face.

"So, awkward question," Marie said. "You're here so soon after I asked you to check out the location in Ogunquit. I assume you didn't go?"

"Oh, I went, all right. As luck would have it, I've got a window of four days before my next engagement. I figured I'd make a day trip of it. I was only about three and a half hours away when you called, so it wasn't so bad."

"I'm sorry…did you say your next *engagement?*"

"I thought it would sound less pretentious than *conference.* I realize now that it did not."

"Anything worth finding?" she asked.

"Um, that's putting it mildly. Were you about to go to bed? I'd love to talk to you about it."

"No, I don't think I could go to bed if I even wanted to."

"Bad day?"

"*Weird* day is a more accurate way of putting it. Tell you what, I'll put on some tea and we can exchange stories."

"Sounds great. Can I rent a room for the next day or so? I'll put my stuff down and freshen up a bit while I wait on the tea."

Marie was more than happy to rent him out a room. Not only did she need the business but she had apparently missed him more than she had realized. It was so good to have him back in the house, to have someone who was accustomed to the obscure and strange to talk to.

With Brendan checked in and lavender chamomile tea steeping, they met back in the sitting room. Marie noticed at once how comfortable Brendan seemed as he sat in the armchair across from her.

"Before I get into things in Ogunquit, fill me in on what's been going on with you," Brendan said. "I can't imagine what it's like to be a murder suspect twice in under three months."

"Well, I think it's the same as last time. The cops have me listed as a suspect. I get the sense that at least Miles is fairly certain it wasn't me, but they just don't have quite enough evidence to remove me from their list of suspects."

"So what exactly has happened?"

She sipped from her tea, took a deep breath, and told him. She started with describing her idea to confront Decker, repeating a few things she had already told him on the phone. She then went into finding the body, having Rick Minor, the real estate agent, find her in a compromising position, and her own personal search for any other

Decker properties. It took a little too long to tell it all; her tea was nearly cold by the time she was through.

"You and Boo just can't stay out of trouble, can you?" Boo, lying at Brendan's feet, lifted his head slightly at the mention of his name.

"It doesn't seem that way." She shrugged and downed the rest of her cold tea. "Okay, so tell what you learned in Ogunquit."

"The housing development was easy enough to find even without an address. There were only eleven homes. Really nice places, with large back yards and immaculate landscaping. I didn't do any market research or anything, but I'm fairly certain all of those houses were very expensive. Anyway, there wasn't really anything subtle about my approach. In fact, I told a little fib to each person I spoke to."

"How little?"

"I told them who I was and what I did for a living. I told them about the TV show and some of the YouTube stuff I'd done. Out of the five people I met, three of them were very happy to speak to me. One pretty much slammed the door in my face—but not out of being annoyed. They looked scared, truth be told. And the fifth one told me that they thought paranormal shows were a scam and I should be ashamed of myself."

"Yikes."

Brendan shrugged. "I've gotten much worse criticism than that in the past. Anyway, three people out of five...I suppose everyone else was away at work. But those three people had some very interesting stories. One woman told me about the imaginary friend her son has...an imaginary friend that she is fairly certain plays harmless pranks around the house. Moving the remote, turning lights on and off, things like that. She said she's seen something a few times. A small shape, about the same size as her son. She told me it's pretty creepy, but she's never felt scared, per se. I asked how long she's experienced things and she said it's been about two and a half years—ever since they moved in.

"The second person I spoke to was an older man. Retired, a widower. He says he's never really *seen* anything, but he heard whispering sometimes. The way he explained it, he'd always just put it out of his mind. He says he'll hear something or just get this cold, strange feeling about two or three times a month. But he said because he's getting up there in age, he figured it might just be his body and mind responding to the loneliness of the house."

Whispering…it made Marie think of Jackson Wallace and the stories of the Union soldier Mrs. Clark had told her about.

"And what about the third person you spoke to?" she asked.

Brendan sat forward, his eyes wandering. "The third story was bad. A middle-aged married couple that are actively trying to sell the house. They claim to wake up at least a few times a month to the sound of someone screaming. The screams seem to come from the downstairs bathroom—a room that they claim is always bitterly cold. There's also moving furniture, scratching noises, full-figured apparitions—what people in my line of work refer to as shadow people—odd smells…"

"Okay, that's enough," she said. "I don't need to hear any more."

She wasn't sure where her mind had insisted it was too much. Likely either at the odd smells or the so-called *shadow people.*

"Well, one other thing you *should* maybe hear. When they started working towards placing their house on the market three months ago, guess who contacted them about buying it."

"Avery Decker."

"Bingo. The husband said he did not want to deal with Decker, though. He thinks Decker might have known the state of the house when he sold it to them—yeah, he's the one who sold it to them in the first place and now wanted to buy it back for less than they bought it for. The husband felt like Decker might have pulled a fast one on them. They both said they are trying to be honest about the situation with the other Realtors that come to the place. The wife said one of the three Realtors they've spoken with has left the house terrified. She asked to use the restroom, then came out and made a quick exit. She allegedly looked as white as a sheet."

"So based on what you found out today and the connections I've made here, wouldn't you agree that it's safe to say Decker was almost seeking out these sort of flawed properties?"
"Without a doubt. And sure, I guess a sleazy businessman would see it as a smart business move. But these are people's lives…"

"And my thinking is that someone he wronged by not disclosing such information might have been so badly affected that they may have wanted revenge."

"I'd say it's a possibility," Brendan said. "But murder?"

"Normally I'd say it seemed like a stretch, too. But when you've lived through an investigation where a man was killed via hot air balloon tampering, you're suddenly willing to consider just about anything."

"So where do we start?" Brendan asked. "Like I said, I've got a few days so I'm more than happy to help."

"I'm not sure yet. Oh…but I should probably tell you that I went to another house with Boo. Ran some more ghosts away."

"You mean *other* than Mrs. Clark?"

"Yeah. A man named Wallace Jackson. Oh, and then Boo also ran some ghosts out of another woman's house when I was visiting to ask questions about Decker."

"Just like that? Knock-knock, hey, how are you, and then sic Boo on some ghosts?"

Just like that," she said with an uneasy smile.

Brendan looked down at the dog, amazed and maybe a little scared. Marie understood the reaction completely. "Jeez…do you have any other secrets you're keeping from me?"

"Actually, yes. But I'll show you in the morning. All this super pleasant conversation, and I've lost track of time."

"Hey, it *is* pleasant conversation for me. I could talk about ghosts and hauntings all day."

"Oh, I know," Marie said with a chuckle. "That's why I'm calling it a night. See you in the morning, Brendan."

"You can't just dangle a surprise and expect me to wait until the morning."

She gave him a smile that she supposed bordered on flirting and said, "And that just makes me want to wait even more."

With that, she left the sitting room. As she made her way down the hall, Boo remained by Brendan's side, but that was okay. She knew Brendan's eyes were still on her and for now, that was enough to send her to sleep happy.

CHAPTER EIGHTEEN

The following morning, Marie found Brendan and Posey already in the dining room, sipping on coffee and eating some of Posey's walnut cinnamon rolls. Posey seemed quite happy that Brendan was there. When Marie sat down to join them, shoveling one of the cinnamon rolls onto her plate, Posey gave her the usual raised-eyebrow look of encouragement. It seemed to ask: *So, are you going to go for this or not?*

"I wasn't expecting a new guest when I arrived here this morning," Posey commented.

"I wasn't expecting one last night, either," Marie said, giving Brendan a playfully evil look.

"What can I say?" Brendan said. "I like to keep people on their toes."

"Good thing I had already planned on making these walnut cinnamon rolls," Posey said. She gave them both a smile and then made no attempt whatsoever at subtleness as she got up and left the room. Even the way she left the dining room and headed into the kitchen—with a little sway in her step—told them that she was intentionally making sure they were being left alone.

"Did you sleep well?" Marie asked.

"I did, actually. I really like this place. I won't go so far as to say it feels like home, but it did feel more familiar than I was expecting."

"That's nice to hear," she said, then took a bite out of her cinnamon roll. The taste was almost too much. She'd had them before but had forgotten how amazing they were.

"So, I want to show you something," Brendan said. "I don't think you're going to like it, but you need to see it, I think."

"Oh no…"

Brendan frowned as he pulled put his phone and opened up Twitter. He scrolled to a few different tweets, showing her each one. As she glanced at them, he summed up what they all said. "I don't know where the source originated, but news about you being a murder suspect is spreading even more. On Twitter in particular, it's spreading like a virus."

"I still can't understand how my name is still even floating around online."

"Like I said...the paranormal community are loyal. There are the UFO nuts, of course—they're just absolutely solid and hang on to every single word published about the topic, right down to the names of people who saw spaceships in the 1940s. But the paranormal community is almost as bad. Whether you like it or not, you're always going to be something of a footnote in supernatural lore now."

"You say that like it's a good thing."

"Well, it's not a *bad* thing. In fact, I think if you ever went public with this thing you and Boo are doing, it'll not only save some face in terms of how the online community sees you, but you'd sort of be legendary."

"I'm not looking to be legendary," she said. She let out a nervous laugh and added: "I just don't want people to think I'm a killer."

"Well, from what you told me last night, it seems like you're working towards proving that...again. So if the ghost-busting stuff doesn't work out, maybe you have a future as a private investigator."

"I don't think that's the best occupation for a forty-year-old woman to just all of a sudden pick up. Besides...if I can figure out how to book these rooms, I think I'm going to really like the whole bed-and-breakfast thing."

Brendan finished off his cinnamon roll and pointed at her. "Oh, and speaking of things we talked about last night, you said you had a secret, right? Something you wanted to show me?"

"Yes," she said. "And you know, I think showing you first thing in the morning would be a great way to kick off the day." She took one more bite of her cinnamon roll, picked up her coffee, and waved him on to follow her. "This way..."

She led him out of the dining room, through the sitting room, and up the stairs. When they passed by Atticus Winslow's room, she made a shushing gesture. Brendan gave her a thumbs-up sign as they passed. When she finally had him in the bedroom on the end of the hall, she felt herself tensing up a bit.

"Looks like a bedroom," Brendan said. "Very similar to the one I am currently staying in."

"Yes, smartypants. But step into the closet. Tell me what you see."

He gave her a wary look but did as he was asked. The moment he was standing inside the doorframe to the closet, he paused. He then turned and looked at her. "Did you have this installed?"

"No. It's been there. Benjamin found it."

"A haunted manor with a hidden room? I tell you…if you were to let me run with the marketing for this place, you'd never have an empty room." He looked back toward the hidden room and asked: "Can I go inside?"

"Yeah," she said, following behind him.

As she filed into the hidden room after him, she realized just how small it was. She watched as Brendan looked to the book on the table, and then to the walls and the ceiling.

"Ever heard of that book?" Marie asked.

Brendan looked back at the book. He carefully ran his hands along the pages and then looked at the cover. "*Do the Dead Believe in Ghosts?* You know, the title does sound familiar, but the book itself is nothing I'm familiar with. Have you looked through it?"

"I almost did. But as I started looking, I found something else. Pictures…of my mother and my aunt. I sort of got sidetracked."

"Understandably so." Brendan flipped through a few pages, finally settling on the table of contents. "There's stuff about séances in here. Some scientific research on the existence of the soul…and the copyright page says it was printed in 1937. So this is an *old* book."

Marie stepped closer to the book and scanned the table of contents. Some of the chapter names made her shudder. *Contacting the Dead. The Other Side. Letting Them In.* She turned the page, and then another and another. Pictures of her mother were still stuck between random pages. Old and worn photographs that told stories about a part of her life she had never dared to ask too much about.

"This book in a hidden room does make me wonder what sort of stuff your Aunt June might have been into," Brendan said. "And it would certainly shed a lot of light on why the place seemed to have been haunted."

"I swear, I never thought Aunt June was into anything dark and gloomy like this," she said, still flipping through the pages of the book. "And even if I did, I would—"

She stopped as she came to another postcard. It was one she had not seen before, tucked away with a few other pictures closer to the back of the book. She took them out and saw that the postcard was from Nome,

Alaska. She turned it over and saw a very brief note. Before she read it, she glanced at the To line (Aunt June) and the From line (Marie's mother).

"Everything okay?" Brendan asked.

"Yeah. Just found something my mom wrote to Aunt June and…oh…oh my God."

Without realizing she was doing so, she pulled the little chair out from under the table and sat down.

"What is it?" Brendan asked.

"My mother…she sort of disappeared off the face of the planet twenty-five years ago. I never knew if she was dead or just decided to walk away from her family. She went missing and we never got any answers…"

"Oh, Marie, I had no idea." His voice was soft and caring, filled with more emotion than she had ever heard out of him.

"That was twenty-five years ago, Brendan. Not a word from her. But this postcard…"

She placed it on top of the book and pointed to the postmark in the corner.

It had been mailed just eleven years ago.

"She was alive," Marie said, closing in on tears. "She was alive, and sending postcards to Aunt June. And Aunt June…she never told me. She lied to me the entire time."

CHAPTER NINETEEN

It was clear that Brendan had no idea how to react to such a revelation, or to a clearly emotional woman. But that was fine with Marie. She was too absorbed in the postcard. She read the brief letter on the back slowly and with great intention, trying to draw some sort of clue out of every word.

June,
It's beautiful here. Been a while since I wrote, and wanted to just check in. I'm still alive and kicking (and maybe in love, too...not sure). And though it is beautiful here, I don't think I've found "it" yet...whatever it is. Miss you tons! Please let Marie know I miss her and I love her. Thanks, June! You're the best!
Love from afar,

The second time she read it, Marie's hands were trembling. She tried to start reading it a third time but could not see through the haze of tears in her eyes. She set the postcard down, wiped her eyes, and instantly started looking for anything else new—anything else that might expose the lie she had been told for so long.

"Marie, are you okay?" Brendan asked.

She shook her head. She found a few more pictures she had missed the other day, but there were no more postcards from her mother. No more letters, no clues of any kind to support the fact that her mother had indeed been alive eleven years ago.

When she found nothing new, she picked up the book by the spine. She shook it, letting all of the pictures and cards fall out. The binding, weak and worn from age, cracked and released a few stray pages.

"Marie, hey…"

It took the sound of Brendan's voice for her to realize that she was still shaking it. And she was shaking with fury, on the brink of a full-on weeping fit.

Slowly, Brendan reached out and took the book from her. He set it on the table and slowly, with the caution he might use in picking up an expensive crystal vase, he drew her in to him. She did not hesitate at all. She let him hug her and cried lightly on his shoulder. She wasn't even sure why she was crying. If anything, she should be angry. She should be angry at June for keeping such a secret from her—angry at her mother for abandoning her family. Now that there was no mystery to it—now that she *knew* her mother had always been alive, but had chosen to leave her family—she knew she had the right to be angry.

But instead, there were only tears. She wasn't sure how to feel. Being so emotionally wrecked inside of a house she had revered in her mind since a child *and* feeling betrayed by a woman she had given godlike status…it was all a bit much.

"I have to get out of here," Marie said. She tore herself away from Brendan (which was harder to do than she cared to admit) and hurried out of the room. She made a beeline straight through the bedroom and out into hallway. She heard Brendan following closely behind her, but his concern for her was the furthest thing from her mind.

By the time she reached the bottom of the stairs, she started to feel better. For a moment there, it had gotten almost hard to breathe, as if the walls were closing in on her. Which, in a house with hidden rooms, she thought might not be entirely out of the question.

She went to the sitting room but rather than sit down, she started to pace. Her brain wanted to latch on to this new mind-blowing information. But everything else within her was resisting it. She knew if she settled in with this new revelation, it would occupy her every thought and make an already crazy few days a living nightmare. So while she knew this new development in the mystery of her mother was certainly worth investigating, it could not be done right now. Right now, she had more than enough to worry about.

"You okay, Marie?" Brendan asked.

He had come slowly down the stairs and was now standing in the entryway to the sitting room. She gave him what she knew was a very weak and forced smile and nodded. "I'll be fine. I just can't take that on right now. Not on top of everything else that's going on."

She appreciated how Brendan was handling it. He was not keeping his distance, terrified of his crying friend. But he also wasn't giving her the *there-there* spiel and a bunch of meaningless pats on the back. He was doing the perfect thing: he was simply being there.

"Sorry if I made your life harder by pointing out all of the social media stuff," he said.

She wiped away an errant tear and sighed. "Oh, I'm really not even worried about that right now. I'm not too worried about what people that don't even know me think of me."

"That must be nice."

Slowly, he stepped into the room. Marie sort of hoped he was going to hug her again. He did no such thing, though. Even if he'd wanted to, Boo came trotting into the room and stood in front of him. In a childlike way, Brendan sat down on the floor and stroked Boo's head.

"So tell me what I can do for you," Brendan said. "Do we ignore this, do we carry on as if it didn't happen?"

"That would be great. For now, anyway. So if you want to do something for me, you can figure out what our next step would be in terms of learning more about Avery Decker and the properties he was swooping in to buy."

"As it so happens, I thought about that last night as I was getting into bed. I just happen to have some of my equipment in my trunk. I think the best step to take in clearing your name is to find out if the house Decker was killed in was allegedly haunted. You said it was a property he was looking to buy, right?"

"Right. And according to Mrs. Clark—an older local lady with her finger on the pulse of county-wide gossip—there's some particularly disturbing history around the land and the house itself."

"So I say start there. If the place is legitimately haunted and we can figure out the property history, maybe there are some answers there." He hesitated and then added: "That is, of course, if you think you'd be up to it."

"Or if we can even get into it," Marie said. "I'm pretty sure Deputy Miles and especially Sheriff Jenkins are very suspicious of me. I wouldn't be surprised if they've got a car on patrol in the area just to make sure I don't decide to swing by."

"We'll cross that bridge when we get there," Brendan said. "What do you say? Want to take me out to that house?"

"I say it's better that sitting around here, waiting."

"And it's even better with some of Posey's cinnamon rolls. Hold on while I grab a few for the road."

She watched as Boo followed Brendan into the dining room, where the remainder of Posey's rolls still waited. As Posey handed him some Tupperware to put them in, a slight noise from behind Marie caused her to turn. She spotted Atticus Winslow coming to the bottom of the stairs. When he saw that Marie had spotted him, he hurried his pace a bit as he headed straight for the front door.

"Good morning, Mr. Winslow," Marie said as cheerfully as she could.

Mr. Winslow gave a very curt nod and raised his hand. She did not think it was a wave, but more of the sort of sign a parent might give a child who would not be quiet. He did not even so much as look at her as he made his way out the front door.

Brendan approached from behind, already munching on one of the cinnamon rolls. "Who was that?"

"That was Mr. Atticus Winslow. He's booked a room for an indefinite amount of time."

"Well, he seems very nice."

Marie couldn't help but laugh. And before she knew it, a comment slipped out of her mouth, one she typically would have kept to herself. "I'm glad you're here, Brendan."

He seemed surprised, but gave her a smile—the sort of warm smile she had not seen out of him ever since they'd met. "Me, too," he said. "Now...let's go check out that house."

CHAPTER TWENTY

The house looked different somehow when Brendan parked in front of it. Marie recalled it looking somewhat strange when she had come here to meet with Decker, but now it looked almost normal. This changed, however, when she glanced around the side of it as she got out of the car. Recalling the stories Mrs. Clark had shared about the property made the place take on an entirely different feel.

Boo jumped out of the car behind her. He sniffed at the ground and then looked up at Marie as if to say: *"What are we doing back here?"*

"Well, it doesn't *look* haunted," Brendan said as they walked toward the house. "Then again, there are very few that ever really do."

Brendan was carrying a small backpack with him, slung over his shoulder. He'd done his best to describe the equipment he'd be using and though most of it went over her head, she got the gist of it. He had something that would be able to pick up thermal images—the shapes and presences of anything using up energy that was invisible to the naked eye. He also had a high-end voice recorder that would pick up noises that the human ear could not. Those two items, along with the help of Boo's talents, were all they had at their disposal—though Brendan said it would be more than enough to get a good gauge of the property.

It also made it much harder that they would not be able to get inside the house. Being that the house was currently for sale and had been vacant for so long, she wasn't even sure who would have had the key. Decker had apparently used one on the day she'd come to pay him a visit, but there was no telling where that was now.

Marie was banking on the property itself, though. If the stories of the stretch of field behind the house were true, then it seemed to her that would be where any activity might occur. Besides…even if she did manage to find a key, she wasn't sure she was quite ready to walk inside a house uninvited. She wasn't even sure who technically owned the house. She supposed that might be one of the next things to look into.

As they reached the house, it was another of those times where Marie felt rather useless—almost in the way. Brendan had his gadgets, and Boo...well, Boo was Boo. The only thing she felt she could add to the equation was an overall sense of being creeped out and being able to respond with goosebumps. These were not exactly the best tools of the trade.

She left Brendan alone and made a slow circuit around the house. She called Boo to follow after her and he did so eagerly. It was almost like he knew why they were there. As he sniffed around the edges of the house, he seemed to be focused on something more than just the typical doggy-sniffing. He wasn't just taking in the scents of a new place; he seemed to be looking for something specific.

And whatever that something was, he did not seem to be finding it at all. In fact, he did not pause or even slow down until they reached the back of the house. When the field came into view, Marie did her best not to be influenced by the stories Mrs. Clark had shared with her.

"There's a field somewhere out there in Amber Hills that hunters swear just gives them the willies during deer season. My husband said the few times he'd been by that field, he'd get the sweats. Felt like there was someone watching him..."

She thought of that poor Civil war soldier, already traumatized in the war and losing his mind. It made her feel uneasy and she—

Boo stopped all of a sudden, his head perking up. He went absolutely rigid, his head pointed out in the direction of the field. Marie turned in that direction as well, though she did it slowly. She wasn't too sure if she wanted to see whatever had Boo so spooked.

But she did look and there *was* something out there. She could just barely see it, a bit further out in the tall weeds. Something dark, staring right back at her.

Marie felt gooseflesh break out on her arms. She could not see what the shape was, but she could *feel* it looking at her. Boo started to growl slightly and when he did, the shape moved.

When it did, Marie felt like a fool.

It was a young deer that had been frozen in fear by the dog and the crazy woman by the house. Marie had been unable to see the entire shape of it while it was in the tall weeds and overgrowth, but once it started leaping back toward the scraggly forest, the shape was clear to see.

"Well, that was embarrassing," Marie said to Boo. "But I won't tell Brendan how scared I was if you won't."

Boo seemed perfectly fine with this arrangement as he started sniffing again. He did so almost casually now, as if he sensed that there was nothing out of the ordinary on this property. When they made it back around to the front of the house, she saw Brendan tinkering with his little EMF audio recorder on the front porch.

He look up at Marie and Boo and frowned. "Did Boo not find anything interesting?"

"Just a spooky deer out in the back field," Marie answered.

Brendan seemed a little disappointed at this but gave a shrug. "We're really doing ourselves a disservice by not being able to enter the house. But honestly, based on the history you've told me about the place, I would have no issue believing the place was haunted if someone claimed it."

"That's just it," Marie said. "We don't know for sure. We've only ever heard anything about the field."

"Well, if you don't mind, for the sake of consistency, I'd like to grab a few minutes of audio. If there *is* something here, I think we've been here long enough to have irritated it. Give me about fifteen minutes, would you?"

"Of course. Might as well, while we're here."

She left Brendan to his work, a little shaken that she was already starting to find this sort of thing normal now. Even when Brendan started slowly marching across the porch, asking questions to any potential entities, she wasn't all that unsettled by it.

"Is it okay that we're here?" he asked. He then waited about twenty seconds and added: "How long have *you* been here? Do you like it here?"

Marie sat on the hood of the car with Boo sniffing around a nearby tree. She started to wonder how to find out who Avery Decker had been talking to about the potential purchase of the house. There was no signage of any kind on the property, making her think the potential sale to Decker had been quite close to being finalized. And if it had been unoccupied for a while—even if it was just a few months—she felt certain a listing would not be hard to find.

On a whim, Marie pulled out her phone and typed the address of the house into a Google search. Several results popped up, including a listing for the property on Zillow. She opened it up and scrolled through the information. While the property was listed as *not for sale*, there was a link at the bottom, titled Associated Listings. She clicked that and saw exactly what she had been hoping to find: up until three weeks ago, the house had been listed with Coastal Gems Realty.

While she waited for Brendan to get enough audio samples, she tried to figure out how to approach a visit to Coastal Gems. It was going to seem strange asking for information about a property Avery Decker had just died in. It would also likely not help that Mr. Minor—the man who had walked into the house to find her crouched over Decker's body—was an agent with Coastal Gems.

Maybe I should drop it, she thought. *Maybe I should just let the cops handle it before I make things any worse.*

On its face, this seemed like a very good idea. But there were aspects to the case that the cops were simply not going to take seriously—namely the fact that the houses Decker was hunting down were haunted.

She pondered these things as Brendan continued to ask questions of an invisible audience. And the question that kept popping up over and over again was a simple one, but with a rather difficult answer: *How do I keep getting into these situations?*

Before she could ruminate too much on this, Brendan was heading back toward the car. There was a confused look on his face. He was wearing a pair of noise cancelling headphones, apparently listening to something from this recording session. He was holding the EVP recorder as he got into the car.

He gave her a *wait-a-sec* gesture and then slid his headphones off. He offered them to her and said: "Tell me what you think."

Marie took the headphones a little awkwardly and hated that she felt creeped out when she slid them on. "What is it?" she asked.

"I don't want to say. I don't want to influence you."

She positioned the headphones over her ears and watched as Brendan cycled through the audio footage. When he stopped, she could hear his voice, very pronounced through the headphones.

"How long have you been here? Do you like it here?"

There was something like very faint static following this, the sound of silence magnified. And then, as gentle as a whisper, there was a response.

"Lonely. Please…help…"

Marie couldn't help it; she took the headphones off quickly and shook her head. "I don't suppose you're trying to play a prank on me, are you?"

He shook his head. "No. So I take it you heard it?"

"Yes."

Brendan looked at her as if he wanted to say something to make her feel better. The thing was that she wasn't sure how she felt. Scared, sure. But something about that voice, so distant and cold, so sad...it almost broke her heart.

"Lonely..."

It sent a shiver through her.

In the end, Brendan did the best thing he could do. He tried to push them on, to get her mind off of it. "So...where to now?"

"Coastal Gems," she said, looking back to the house. "Turns out they had their eyes on it at the same time Decker was trying to take it over."

"So they were wanting to grab it up, too?"

"Seems like it. But the agent that found me over his body...he was there to meet with Decker. I can't remember why...maybe they were supposed to be finalizing the sale? Work something out, maybe?"

Brendan shrugged. "Don't ask me. The only time I care anything about real estate is when there are ghosts living in the houses in question."

"So what do you say?" Marie asked. "Want to keep playing detective with me?"

He started the car as Boo hopped up into the back seat. "Ten-four, partner."

With that, he pulled out of the driveway. As they left, Marie turned to give the place one final look. Something began to resonate inside of her and she wasn't sure how to feel about it.

"Lonely. Please...help..."

Was there yet another side to the supernatural that she didn't understand yet? And, if so, how on earth was she supposed to process it?

CHAPTER TWENTY ONE

The Coastal Gems office was a beautiful building that had been constructed to look like an elaborate beach cabin. There was a wraparound porch with a porch swing and numerous Adirondack chairs. Several potted tropical-looking plants tied it all together. The interior was more of the same. It looked exactly like a massive beachfront home—an image only broken up by the two large desks that sat in the large front room.

One of the desks was vacant, left tidy with a few stacks of pamphlets and brochures in its center. A mousy-looking woman sat at the other desk, looking up at Marie and Brendan as they walked in. She was rather pretty, in a plain sort of way. Bright blue eyes shone from behind a pair of glasses that Marie considered to be librarian-like. Her hair, though in need of a proper brushing, was strawberry blonde and done up in a messy bun.

"Hey there," the woman said. "Can I help you two?"

"Yes, actually," Marie said. "We have a question about a property that doesn't seem to currently have an agent or company listed as selling it. But we do know it's available."

"I can help with that," the woman said, pulling her laptop closer to her and readying her fingers to type. What's the address of the property?"

"It's at two twen—"

"What the hell are you doing here?" a male voice interrupted from their right.

Marie turned and saw a familiar face. It was Rick Minor, the man who had caught her in a very compromising position over the dead and bloody body of Avery Decker.

"I'm looking into—"

"No! Gale, don't you dare answer this woman's questions! For all we know, she killed Avery!"

"Oh," Gale said, looking up from her desk with a scrutiny now. "Is this her? The suspect?"

"Hold on a second," Brendan said. "Marie didn't kill anyone. She didn't even—"

"I walked in and saw her standing over a body that was still leaking blood," Minor said.

"Which I'm sure looked terrible," Brendan said. "But this woman is not a killer."

"So you say," Rick Minor said. "I don't know you, so, of course, will not take your word for it." He then looked directly back at Marie and added: "Back to my main question. Why are you even here? Covering your tracks?"

"No. I wanted to know more about the house he was killed in. I've done some digging and have found a pretty alarming trend in the properties he seemed to have a particular interest in."

"Ma'am, I'm sorry," Gale said. "But even if you weren't a suspect, I wouldn't be able to give you information on that house, as it's not actively ours."

"So it belonged to Decker when he was killed?"

"Well, basically. It was in a transi—"

"No," Minor said, rushing in and standing between Gale and Marie. "Not another word. And Ms. Fortune, if you don't leave the premises right now, we'll call the police."

Brendan took a step forward. He was not very muscular and did not look very threatening in most situations, but he had a few inches on Minor and did a good job of setting his jaw to look intimidating.

"That seems a bit much," Brendan said. "But honestly, if you're going to blow a gasket over it, fine. But you know…maybe you should do some digging yourself. It seemed Avery Decker was interested in purchasing sever—"

"Avery Decker was a friend of mine," Minor said, interrupting yet again. "I was quite sad when he left us to go solo—as most of us here at Coastal Gems were—but he remains a friend. If you are truly digging into his personal matters, it makes me want you out of my sight even further. Now…last warning. Leave now or I *will* call the police."

Brendan looked back at Marie and gave her a little shrug. Marie figured the shrug meant *why waste your time?* She agreed, and turned away without saying anything else. At least now she understood a bit more clearly why Minor had seemed so out of sorts and almost taking things personally on the day they'd both discovered Decker's body.

She and Brendan left as casually as they could. Marie felt much better when they were back outside on the porch. She hadn't realized just how trapped she'd felt inside while Minor had been yelling at her. She breathed in the salty beachfront air and sighed it out. "Well, that was awkward."

"Yeah, but at least you now know that if it wasn't *technically* Decker's property, it was very close to being wrapped up."

She hesitated as they reached Brendan's car. The windows were rolled down, Boo poking his nose out at them. "He seems pretty sure I killed Decker, don't you think?" she asked.

"I don't know. If they were really friends at some point, maybe he's legitimately upset. Maybe he's hoping you killed Decker so it makes sense."

"That house could crack my theory, you know," she said as she opened the passenger side door. "If it's not haunted, then it breaks the chain."

"Not necessarily. Take it from me…someone who knows all about the power of spooky stories. Even if there wasn't any documented haunting activity in that house, the Civil War history you told me about would be enough to affect the population's ideas of a house. And if your friend Mrs. Clark was telling the truth about the reactions of hunters…yeah, I think Decker might have wanted it even without firmly documented cases of a haunting. And besides…you heard that audio."

Marie nodded quickly, not wanting to recall the disembodied voice. She got into the car and was about to close the door when she saw the mousy woman who had greeted them—Gale, she recalled—come rushing out of the front door. She gave a cautious look back, as if to make sure Rick Minor wasn't watching her, before she came down the steps.

"Ms. Fortune, wait," Gale said, her voice lowered but not quite in a whisper.

Curious, Marie got out of the car to join the woman at the bottom of the steps.

"Sorry about Rick," Gale said, sliding her glasses further up her nose with a pointed finger. "He's been very emotional ever since Mr. Decker was killed. But you may be on to something. I've always thought there was something strange about what Mr. Decker was up to ever since he left Coastal Gems."

"Like what?" Marie asked.

Gale once again looked back to the front door. "I don't have time to get into it right now. Can you meet me somewhere later today, after I get off of work?"

"Sure. You know where I live?"

"June Manor, right?"

"Yes. Come by when you get off work."

"It'll be a bit later than that," Gale said, already heading back up the stairs. "I have some errands to run after work. How about eight o'clock?"

Before Marie could even get out "Sounds great," Gale was already running back up the stairs.

Brendan looked over the hood of the car at her. "When was the last time you had just a normal day?" he asked. "No deaths, no murder investigations, no people highly suspicious of you?"

"Oh, it's been a while."

He nodded and said, "It's sort of exciting, isn't it?"

"You and I have different definitions of exciting."

They shared a nervous little laugh as they got back into the car and left Coastal Gems Realty. Marie felt like she'd gotten a lot accomplished so far today, but had gotten no answers to show for it. And when it came down to her, a non-local, once again trying to clear her name, those weren't exactly the results she was looking for.

CHAPTER TWENTY TWO

Posey and Marie were putting up the night's leftovers when there was a gentle knock at the front door. Boo was the first at the door, sniffing at it and pawing at the bottom, looking back to the slow humans to see what the hold-up might be. Marie answered the door and greeted Gale as warmly as she could, given the situation.

When Gale stepped inside, the look on her face was similar to the one Marie had seen on the faces of just about every guest she'd welcomed. There was awe and surprise, but an underlying hint of puzzlement.

"What a gorgeous place," Gale said.

"Thanks. It's finally starting to feel like home. But in terms of a bed-and-breakfast I suppose I could be doing much better. Would you like the tour?"

Gale considered it for a moment, grinning as she looked up the entryway staircase. "No, I shouldn't. I already feel a little strange even being here. Rick would freak out. No offense or anything, but the faster I can make this, the better I'm going to feel."

"Is he your boss?"

"No, but he's on the fast track to it. When Decker left Coastal Gems two years ago, Rick was given a lot of his workload and he excelled at it. Despite your opinion of him based on today, he's a very good agent and a hard worker."

"Well, come on out to the back porch," Marie said. "I don't really have an office, so it's what I've been using since I've been here."

Marie led her out onto the back porch, passing through the kitchen where Posey and Brendan were drinking wine; Posey was complaining about summer coming to an end and how dead Port Bliss would be when the tourists were gone. Marie cringed inside, as she knew it would be just one more obstacle to making sure she could keep guests in June Manor.

"Brendan, would you like to join us?" Marie asked. She wanted him to hear whatever Gale had to say, especially if he planned to help her out from this point on. Plus, she figured he might need rescuing from

Posey who, once she got going on a topic, was very hard to remove from it.

"Right behind you," he said, giving an apologetic look to Posey.

The three of them walked out onto the back porch. Dusk was thickening into something darker as true night was only about twenty minutes away. Gale took a moment to take in the scenery, a smile touching her thin lips.

"This is a beautiful view," she commented. "Your guests are lucky."

"My guests are also few and far between," Marie said. She wished she'd kept the remark to herself once it was out. She was starting to understand that she was not only being too hard on herself, but making others feel that she might be throwing one big pity party for herself. She leaned against the rail as Gale settled into the bench of the picnic table. "So…what did you want to tell me?"

"Well, first of all, I don't think you killed Avery. If it was as cut and dry as Rick is making it seem, you'd have been arrested by now. Also, quite frankly, you don't seem like the type."

"Thanks for that."

"Secondly, I did notice that a few of the properties Avery was picking up once he left Coastal Gems seemed to have a weird history to them. He bought one just outside of town where a man committed suicide in the late eighties, up in the attic. Then there was another house out in Amber Hills that he bought cheap, demolished, and built this gorgeous Colonial on it. Before he purchased it, the house had been vacant. It once belonged to a man that, rumor has it, served twenty years in prison for setting fire to his brother's house. There are others, of course. There's the big place in Ogunquit, and the rentals outside of Amber Hills. All of them have some sort of sordid history."

"I've been to a few of them in the last few days…before he was killed. I wanted to meet with him to ask about it."

"Now, from a business standpoint, if we're being honest, it's a smart move. Shady, sure. Maybe even a little mean. But it's smart. And even though a lot of agents and land developers around here will say they had a bad feeling about him from the start, it's mostly jealousy— jealousy from not having the guts to do what he did."

"Forgive me if this sounds ignorant," Brendan said, "but what exactly was he doing?"

Marie appreciated the gesture; he was getting someone who knew Avery personally to admit to what she had been suspecting. It was a genius move, making her wonder how often he'd used it in his odd profession.

"He was buying up what are considered stigmatized properties," Gale said. "He'd approach the owners, pointing out all the reasons they were sitting on a flawed property. And once he'd scared them a bit, he'd convince them to sell at a low-ball price. Once the sell was finalized, he'd either tear the homes down or severely remodel them into much more expensive properties and sell them off—sometimes to individuals, and sometimes to real estate firms. On that Amber Hills deal alone, I know for a fact he netted about four hundred grand—and that's not including the cut he gets on the monthly rental fees."

"He had his eyes on my house for that very same purpose," Marie said. "It's how I met him, in fact. Two days before he died, he was standing in my foyer, trying to bully me into selling the place."

"That sounds like Avery, all right."

"I called a few other owners of houses that were…well, that were allegedly haunted or flawed in some way."

"Haunted?" Gale asked.

"Yes," Marie said, a little embarrassed. "Note, I said *allegedly*. And you know what, though. Both of the people I spoke with had interactions with Avery. One purchased her home from him and claimed it was haunted afterwards—that Mr. Decker knew about it and never disclosed it. The other stated that Mr. Decker tried to buy his property…which was also allegedly haunted."

"Haunted," Gale said, pronouncing the word as if it was a foreign language.

Marie only gave a shrug. There was no way she'd be able to explain the complexities of it all to her.

"So what about the house he was killed in?" Brendan asked. "Was he after it because of the spooky Civil War stories?"

"I'd assume so. That house has been a beast to even get anyone to look at for the last few years."

"Gale, have the police spoken with you?" Marie asked.

"They have. But they were more interested in what Rick had to say because of his position with the agency. Also because he was there shortly after Avery was killed."

"Given that," Marie said, "please forgive me for asking what is going to seem like a very police-like thing to ask. But…do you know if there was anyone Mr. Decker had crossed? Maybe someone that might consider him an enemy?"

"That list would include anyone he purchased land from, I would think. Although I guess *enemy* might be too strong of a word. But really, if there's anyone that stands out, it's a guy named Beau Fowler. He's another property developer. He doesn't really work around Port Bliss much. He's more in tune with properties in Amber Hills, Sutton, and towns like that. But he and Avery used to butt heads over properties when Avery was working with Coastal Gems. I feel like things likely got worse between them when Avery went solo. I'm pretty sure Fowler got beat out by Avery on those Amber Hills rentals. There was some arguing between the two of them and from what I understand, Fowler threatened to go public with information that people had died on that land."

"Was there any truth to it?" Brendan asked.

"Apparently, because to beat Fowler to the punch, Avery made the announcement himself. He disclosed the information and then bought the property at a reduced cost. So Fowler's little threat backfired."

"You know this guy personally?" Marie asked.

"No. I mean, I've met him a few times. I tried to keep my distance from him—so did everyone at Coastal Gems for that matter. He was bad-mouthing Avery every chance he got for a while. He was even making sure people knew he had once worked for us, trying to make us look bad, too. He was *mad.*"

"But before the bickering between them, was there any history about the property? About people dying?"

"Or being haunted?" Brendan asked.

"I never heard of it, if so."

The three of them remained in silence for a while. Marie realized she had a viable lead now. One she figured the police might have already uncovered. As she looked out to the ocean, she figured there was only one way to find out.

"Anyway, I've probably said more than too much," Gale said. "And the last thing I want to do is to point fingers at anyone and interfere in a police investigation."

"No worries there," Marie said. "Everything you've told us stays between us."

"I appreciate that," Gale said, heading for the back door.

"Can I get you some tea before you go?" Marie asked.

"No thank you."

Marie felt a little bad for Gale. The woman looked genuinely concerned—perhaps worried she'd said too much. She escorted her to the door, Brendan standing back in the sitting room with Boo.

"I appreciate the information," Marie said as Gale walked through the front door. "And I'm sorry if I made things stressful at work today."

"It's okay. Rick has been very out of sorts ever since Avery died. I think seeing you again just set him off." She looked back beyond Marie's shoulder, into the foyer and hallway beyond. "You really do have a lovely place here."

With that, Gale made her exit, leaving Marie with more information on the so-called stigmatized properties. More than that, she had what seemed to be the most promising lead yet.

CHAPTER TWENTY THREE

It was one of those nights where Marie *knew* she was not going to be able to sleep well. When she settled down for bed, her mind was on the sort of dealing Avery Decker and this other property developer Beau Fowler had been seeking out. More than that, she wondered how her Aunt June had turned Decker away, and if she'd had any dealings with Fowler.

And when she thought of June, her mind went to the new discoveries she'd made about her own personal life. June had known her mother was alive at least eleven years ago but had failed to say anything to her. She had been keeping secrets. That, of course, raised the question of *why?* That brought up thoughts of the hidden room and the postcards and the book. And that brought up even more questions piled on top of more questions.

When she finally fell asleep around 1:30 in the morning, it did not take her long to fall into a strange dream. To call it a nightmare would have been too dramatic, but it was much more than a dream.

In it, she was sitting on the beach with Avery Decker. The sun was setting and the crabs had come out, inspecting the sand.

"I know you didn't do it," Decker told her.

"Who did?" she asked him.

He only shrugged. He then picked up a crab and threw it as far as he could out into the water. "You don't need to be involved in every tragedy in this town, Marie," he said. Only somehow, Decker was no longer sitting there. Now it was her mother—Abigail Fortune. Only, it was the Abigail that Marie had seen in the pictures she'd found in the old book. When Marie saw the bump on her mother's stomach indicating that she was pregnant, she giggled.

"Why'd you leave?" Marie asked.

"Because I was a stigmatized property."

"You left me and Dad and when he died...I miss you, Mom."

"I know. But now you're finding all the hidden things. Just be careful, okay. Sometimes things hidden should not be found."

With that, her mother started laughing. When she tilted her head back and cackled, a crab started to work its way out of her mouth. Marie looked away and when she did, she saw Boo farther down the beach. He was digging furiously, sand spraying up into the violet sky.

"No, Boo! Leave it!"

But he did not hear her. He kept digging and digging, not hearing her cries. As she ran to him, something dark came out of the hole and—

"No, Boo!"

She sat up in bed, the words coming out of her mouth like a rogue wind. For a puzzled moment, Marie slapped at her bed, thinking there was a crab crawling its way toward her. As her frantic mind slowly settled, she took a series of deep breaths and listened to the murmured crashing of waves from behind the house.

"Sometimes things hidden should not be found."

Those words from her mother echoed in her head. She glanced to the bedside clock and saw that it was 5:13. She toyed with the idea of trying to get back to sleep but knew it would be useless. Besides, Posey would be tinkering around in the kitchen in about forty-five minutes.

Idly, she also wondered if she might catch a peek of Mr. Atticus Winslow at this early hour. She got out of bed and didn't even bother changing into appropriate clothes. She stepped out in her pajamas: a vintage Care Bears T-shirt and a pair of comfy gym shorts, and headed straight to the kitchen where she put a pot of coffee on.

As she stood there and waited for the brewing to be done, she thought of the day ahead. She knew she'd be paying Beau Fowler a visit. Aside from that, she figured she could reorganize her priorities and pay attention to the house. The list of things for Benjamin to fix was getting smaller and smaller, but she also knew she needed to assess a lot of other things. The back porch would need staining soon, and the edging along the driveway was—

"Any chance I could get some tea?"

She nearly screamed at the male voice from behind her. She turned and saw Atticus Winslow standing in the entryway between the dining room and kitchen. He looked refreshed and somehow renewed—much more alive-looking than when he had checked in. He was wearing a black T-shirt and a black pair of jeans, his hands tucked casually into the pockets.

"Of course," she said. She hurried to the cupboard, got the kettle out, and set it on the stove. "Any particular kind?" she asked.

119

"Anything with ginger would be fine."

There was a strange tone to his voice—not mean, per se, but a dry sort of indifference that made it clear he did not like speaking to people. Marie did everything she could not to strike up conversation. Eventually, she relented and settled on something simple as she plopped a lemon ginger tea bag into a teacup.

"Are you enjoying your stay?" she asked.

"Yes. It's a lovely house and you have done an excellent job of making sure I am not bothered."

"Well, I take the wishes of my guests very seriously."

"Tell me…was this always your home?"

"No sir. I inherited it from my great-aunt."

He nodded, a thoughtful look on his face. "I believe I will require at least two more days added on to my stay. Is that acceptable?"

"Of course. We can—"

The kettle whistled and she took it off the burner at once. As she poured the water into the cup, she continued. "We can settle up the difference later today if that's okay with you."

"Just keep up with what I owe and I shall pay you promptly when I leave."

She handed him his teacup and he gave her a curt nod. He then turned away and headed directly back to the stairs, taking his tea with him without another word. Marie stood there for a moment, not sure what she was feeling. She did not feel uneasy around Winslow, but she *did* feel that something was rather off about the man—his strange need for absolute privacy and silence aside.

Marie poured her coffee and saw that she had another half an hour before Posey arrived—and probably another hour or so before Brendan woke up, based on what she remembered of his schedule from the last time he'd stayed at June Manor.

She knew exactly what she wanted to do but figured she'd give Mr. Winslow an ample head start up the stairs before she moved. She sipped from her coffee in silence for a few minutes and then also went upstairs. She went slowly by Mr. Winslow's room, then by Brendan's room, on her way to the room at the end of the hallway. She opened up the closet and then stepped into the previously hidden room.

She didn't waste time taking in the strangeness of the place. Honestly, the more she stepped into the room, the more natural it felt. Once she got past the fact that it was a *hidden room*, there really wasn't much to it. A table, a chair, dusty walls, and an old forgotten book. Sure, the subject matter of the book creeped her out a bit—especially given that there were pictures and secrets from Aunt June's past tucked within it. But it did not stop her from once again taking the postcards and letters out.

Now that she knew June had actively been keeping secrets about her mother, Marie approached the book with much less reverence. She took the cards and letters out, not caring where they were placed within the book. She made individual piles of the numerous things she found inside: one pile for items that were specifically related to only June, and another pile that either referenced or featured her mother. A June pile and an Abigail pile.

She started with rereading the postcard from her mother, making sure she hadn't simply *made* herself see something of importance on her last visit to the room. But the card read the same and the postmark did indeed prove that it had come eleven years ago. It was enough evidence, she supposed, to prevent her mother from being declared legally dead.

But for what? she asked herself. *It's quite clear she does not want to be found...that she does not want her family.*

She eyed the pictures of her mother, studying closely the one of her with a pregnant belly.

She waited for some overpowering emotion to pop up, but there was none. She wondered if she had simply become desensitized to her mother's absence. Yes, there was some relief in knowing her mother was likely still alive out there in the world somewhere, but the lies negated that relief. So, instead of torturing herself by obsessing over old pictures and what appeared to be proof that her mother was not dead, Marie instead turned her attention to the book itself.

She supposed the book was a different sort of proof. It was proof that June was interested in the paranormal and maybe even the occult. Honestly, this did not surprise Marie nearly as much as news of her mother's postcard from Alaska. It was rather easy to picture June tucking herself away in a hidden room, reading a book about séances and spirits. The question it brought to mind, though, was if she'd known there had been ghosts in her house. And how long she had been interested in the topic.

Also, why hide away in a secret room to read about it when she had an entire gorgeous house at her disposal? She supposed it did make the book a little more mysterious. She started slowly flipping through the pages, not fully understanding everything she was reading.

The Ethereal Realm. Modern science and death. Contacting deceased loved ones. Respecting the setting...

Although she had never been one to stereotype people, Marie couldn't help but feel as if this was a lot of paranormal mumbo jumbo. Yet at the same time, she felt that by even skimming the pages, she was inviting dark things to manifest within the room.

A gentle knock behind her startled her. She turned and saw Brendan standing there with a cup of coffee. "I thought I might find you here."

"Good guess. I'm trying to make sense of it. Why the room exists, what Aunt June might have been into, why she lied about my mother. Why my mother..."

She stopped here, feeling herself getting far too vulnerable in front of Brendan and not liking it.

"You know," Brendan said, "I could look around just to be sure, but I think that book might be worth a lot of money. It's obviously quite old and even as early as the 1930s, occult books were rather hard to come by. They were published, but the print runs were pretty small. It could be a collector's item."

"Don't waste your time. It was obviously important to June...even though it might be a little creepy."

"Can I make an observation?" Brendan asked.

"Is it going to scare me?"

"Maybe."

She rolled her eyes at him and sipped from her coffee. "Yes. But be gentle."

"The book deals with séances and communing with the dead. Traditionally, a séance is supposed to be conducted in a very quiet location where focus is of the utmost importance. No distractions of any kind. Seems to me that this room would have been perfect. So it makes me wonder if your aunt was just reading about them or..."

"...or conducting them," Marie finished.

They both stood in the silence of this thought, the small hidden room suddenly feeling much smaller as far as Marie was concerned. She slowly stepped out of the room, this time taking the letters, pictures, and postcard with her.

Brendan, apparently sensing that she wanted the topic changed, asked: "So are we going to see Mr. Beau Fowler today?"

"Yes. And the sooner the better. Though, you know…I'll again give you the chance to opt out. This is my little quest. You don't have to come along."

"I know. But I sort of enjoy it. After all, there *is* a supernatural element at the core of it all. But if you want to go solo and don't want me along, just say it and I'm a ghost."

"Bad choice of words," Marie said with a grin. "And I love having you tag along. I just don't want you to feel forced into it."

They were at the doorway, about to head back out into the hall, when Brendan turned to face her. He did so rather quickly, making Marie halt in her tracks. They were standing no more than a foot apart, eyes locked. A little flush of heat passed along Marie's face.

"None of this is forced," he said, holding her gaze.

They looked at one another for another few seconds before Brendan gave her a small smile and walked down the hall. Marie stood in the doorway a moment longer, the weight and meaning of his comment settling on her like a very strange hug.

CHAPTER TWENTY FOUR

Beau Fowler owned one of the most beautiful homes Marie had ever seen. It was two stories, with what she had always thought of as a third look-out story on the back half of the house. Even parking in the elaborate paved driveway, Marie and Brendan could already see the amazing view of the beach. Because Fowler's home was a bit removed from the Port Bliss town limits, the beach was less developed, a little more wild-looking.

It was 8:17 when Marie parked her car in Fowler's driveway. She was glad they'd decided to come out early, because they just managed to catch Fowler on his way out. He was placing a briefcase in the front of his truck and a large red toolbox in the back when Marie and Brendan stepped out of her car.

Fowler was a tall, handsome man. He had a face that some would call grizzled while others might use a word like rugged. He had a moustache that harkened back to 1980s detectives and a pair of sunglasses that only added to the appearance. He looked to be about fifty or so and when he regarded Marie and Brendan, he did so with an authentic smile despite the fact that they were strangers who had just parked in his driveway.

"G'morning," he said, his voice thick with an unmistakable northern accent—though his sounded more like Boston than coastal Maine. "Can I help you folks?"

"You're Beau Fowler, correct?" Marie asked.

"That's me. And who might you be?"

"I'm Marie Fortune. I'm somewhat new to Port Bliss and own—"

"You run June Manor, that bed-and-breakfast. Although I've seen it called something else in the news here and there. The Ghostly Grounds, right?"

"Yes, unfortunately, I did get that little tag. How did you know about that?"

"Well, I'm a property developer. So I keep my eye on properties of interest. And while I was indeed very sorry to hear about your Aunt June passing away all those months ago, I do have to admit that I had

124

my eye on that house. Out of respect, I kept my distance. And then when I saw you had turned it into a bed-and-breakfast, I figured it was a lost cause."

"Oh," Marie said, not quite sure how to continue. "Well, thanks for that level of respect."

"Of course. So what can I do for the two of you?"

"Well, I had some questions about a man I understand was something of your rival. Mr. Avery Decker."

"Ah," Fowler said. "Well, I don't know if you've heard but there's not much of a rivalry anymore. Avery died a few days ago. Rumor has it he was murdered right inside a house he was in the process of buying."

"Yes, I know about that," Marie said. "As it happens, I was the person who found his body. And, as you can imagine, I'm being eyed as a suspect."

"That's awful," Fowler said. It seemed as if he meant it; even his moustache seemed to frown on its own. "But I have to go back to my original question: what can I do for you?"

"I recently discovered that you and Decker had something of an argument over a property that has, since then, been referred to as stigmatized."

The jovial expression on his face evaporated. He eyed Marie and Brendan as if they had just called him a particularly nasty name. "Yes, that's accurate. We got into a spat over a property we both believed could make us some money. But in doing research on the property, I discovered that three people had died on the property in the nineties. And yes…we got a little nasty with each other in how we attempted to fight for the property. In the end he took a gamble, outsmarted me, and ended up buying the property at an absolute steal."

"Was that the only time you've ever worked hard to buy a property that you knew was stigmatized?" Brendan asked.

Rather than answer them, Fowler went back to the driver's side door of his truck. Before getting inside, he turned back to them. Marie was glad he was wearing sunglasses; she assumed the look of anger in his eyes might turn her slightly cold.

"Not that it's any of your business, but yes. I tried a few different times to beat Decker at his own game, but was never quite able to. However, I have done very well for myself all along the coast."

He got into his truck and reached for the door. But before he closed it, he had one more thing to say. "I'm not stupid, Ms. Fortune. You say you're being eyed as a suspect and then come to ask questions of a man that had a small feud with him. You want to know if it was me. You want to know if I killed him. I can tell you with absolute clarity that no…I did not kill him. But if you're looking for a killer, I'd maybe look at the people he wronged and ripped off. I hate to speak ill of the dead, but Avery Decker was a cruel bastard when it came to the business side of things. Working with properties with shady histories, I'm sure he eventually came across someone that snapped. So if you're playing amateur detective, that's where I'd start."

"Mr. Fowler," Brendan said. "Look, you have to understand that we—"

"If you'll excuse me, I have work to get done today," Fowler interrupted. "Kindly get off of my property."

With that, he closed the truck door and started the engine. Although the driveway was more than big enough for him to back out without hitting Marie's car, he remained parked, waiting for them to leave first.

"I think we made him mad," Marie said. She said it in a way that was an attempt at humor, but fell flat. If anything, it made her sound nervous.

She backed her car out of his driveway and headed back toward the center of town. "What do you think? Did Fowler seem capable of murder?"

"No clue. But I have this thing where I never underestimate a man with a moustache that looks that awesome."

Marie shook her head, chuckling nervously. She knew that Fowler had a good point—a point she had even considered herself; there was a very good chance that Decker's killer was someone he had wronged. Maybe someone he'd knowingly sold a haunted or otherwise flawed property to.

"Have you ever heard of people snapping and going a little off the rails due to a haunting?" Marie asked.

"Oh yeah. There are stories like that all over the place. Amityville is a good one. And of course, there are tons of killers that confessed to their crimes, but also said the voices in their heads made them do it."

"Do you think he's right? Do you think it could be one of Decker's past c—"

126

Her phone rang, cutting her off. She took the phone from the console and, coming to a stop sign, checked the caller display.

"Ah crap," she said.

"Who is it?"

"It's Deputy Miles."

Of course, she knew the chances that he might be calling with good news were just about as likely as the chances that he had bad news. She figured there was no sense in delaying either, so she answered. She put it on speakerphone so Brendan could listen in.

"Hi, Deputy Miles," she answered.

"Hi, Ms. Fortune. Listen, I've got a few things to go over with you. First and foremost, we got a call from Rick Minor of Coastal Gems yesterday afternoon. He was very upset that you had come by their offices and were asking questions about Avery Decker."

"Sir, there was no way I could have known he'd react in such a way."

"I understand that. But the question remains…why were you there asking about Decker at all?"

It was a question that had many answers—but none that Deputy Miles was going to like. "I'm just trying to figure out what happened. Sir…I get it. I find the man dead not even a full two days after he tried to bully me into selling my house. I understand the scrutiny. I just needed to know why he wanted my house…and why he was tied up in other properties with certain…complexities."

"Ms. Fortune, all of his dealings are coming up in our investigation. And quite honestly, the more questions we ask, the more the rumors are getting spread. And that makes our job so much harder. You have to trust us to make sure your name gets cleared. When you go looking for answers yourself, you're only muddying up the process. You can understand that, right?"

"Yes, sir. I apologize."

"Thank you. Now…I have an update for you that I feel you should be included on. While we still have some forensics experts looking into the scene of the crime, one thing seems to be inescapable. And that's that we can't find a single print anywhere in the house. Not on the door, not the floor, not the stairs, furniture, *nothing*. There were also no prints found on Mr. Decker. However…there was something found on his body that, quite frankly, does not work at all in your favor."

"What's that?" she asked, her heart dropping in her chest.

127

"Two of your hairs, on his shirt."

"Sir, I was leaning right over him and—"

"Yes, we've discussed this already. It could be completely random. However, it doesn't look great in addition to you conducting your own investigation. In fact, it's starting to look worse and worse."

"Okay..."

"Also, while the initial findings supported the idea that he had been stabbed, the coroner now says he can't be too sure. They think he was certainly stabbed, but they have no idea what he was stabbed *with*.

"I tell you all of this because one more break against you, and it might be enough for us to make a formal arrest. And if you *are* innocent, that's the last thing you want to happen. And if we get another call like the one we got from Mr. Minor, I may have to be more firm next time. Am I clear?"

"Yes, sir. Perfectly clear."

"Good. Hopefully I won't have to speak to you again." He paused, as if it had been hard on him to be so strict. Finally, he concluded with, "Goodbye, Ms. Fortune."

With that, Miles ended the call. Marie sighed and shook her head. "Unbelievable. Though, I figured Minor would do something like that."

"Miles seems understanding, though. Maybe seeing how you helped catch two killers the last time you were in trouble has softened him up."

"Maybe. But...no prints of any kind at the scene? No evidence at all? I mean, it almost sounds like a ghost did it."

Brendan looked at her, wide-eyed and with an uneasy smile. "You said it, not me."

CHAPTER TWENTY FIVE

When they returned to June Manor, Marie found Posey in the sitting room with Boo curled up at her feet. She was drinking tea and reading Joseph Conrad's *Heart of Darkness*. Seeing her there, almost as if she were imprisoned in the house, Marie skipped joining her and went to the little basket she kept her bills in, located under the check-in desk in the foyer. She took out her checkbook and wrote the check she'd promised Posey earlier. She wrote it for two thousand dollars. She had plenty in her checking account right now, thanks to payments from Mrs. Grace and Wallace Jackson, but did not want to push it. If things went well financially in the next two weeks or so, she'd gladly write Posey another.

She walked into the sitting room and handed Posey the check. Posey set the book down, took the check, and shook her head. "This is too much."

"Are you kidding? You've been chef and even a lookout when I've gone out to run my crazy errands. After nearly three months of that, you deserve more than this. Please, Posey. Take it."

Posey took the check and pocketed it with a look of gratitude. Behind them, Brendan was tinkering in the kitchen, pouring a cup of coffee. Posey leaned to the right so she could see around Marie, through the dining room and toward the kitchen. She looked back at Marie and said: "So how's *that* going?"

"There's nothing to *go*."

"Oh, yes there is. Just give it time." She chuckled and then, as if the thought had just come to her, she slapped at her knee with her free hand. She grabbed her cell phone from the little reading table by the chair and opened up a text thread.

"Something wrong?" Marie asked.

"No, not wrong. But this Decker guy you've been looking into. Did you know that he was buying houses *after* convincing people that there was something wrong with the house? Telling owners that if they ever wanted to sell, it would be difficult if word ever got out that x, y, or z had happened. Rumor has it he purchased at least three or four properties in such a way and made a pretty penny. Can you imagine what he might have done to *this* house if he'd convinced you?"

"Yes, I did know that. Brendan and I have been learning all about that, actually. But how did *you* find out?"

"My friend Sheryl told me. And I think her hairdresser told her."

"In other words, it's in the gossip mill?"

"Seems like it."

Brendan came into the room with his cup of coffee. He'd apparently heard most of the conversation, as he asked: "Any idea where it might have started?"

"No," Posey said. "Gossip starts with a whisper somewhere, you know? You could ask three different people where a piece of it came from and you're going to get three different answers. And being that Decker was killed, he's a hot topic."

"Posey, when did you hear about it?" Marie asked.

"Oh, just this morning. About two or three hours ago."

Marie turned to Brendan, a frown on her face. "How long do you think it'll be before this hits social media?"

"No clue," he said. "Being that this is a small town in Maine, I'd say we have some time. But if there are real bloodhounds out there interested in you and the B&B, there's no telling."

"Bloodhounds?"

"Yeah," Brendan said, almost apologetically. "Sadly, I can almost guarantee you that editors of online paranormal magazines have either your name or Port Bliss saved as a Google alert. That means whenever Marie Fortune or Port Bliss pops up in a news article or social media post anywhere online, they'll be notified. It's sort of like Posey's gossip mill in that it starts slow and innocent. But instead of two ladies exchanging it over texts, these people pop it out to tens of thousands in one fell swoop."

While this prospect was certainly alarming, it brought to mind another question. Until yesterday, it seemed that Decker's dirty dealings were a well-buried secret that she had just happened to uncover. But now it seemed it was quickly becoming common knowledge. Between her puny investigations and the work the police were doing, had someone been so stirred up as to put Decker's sordid business practices on blast?

"We need to get in front of this," Marie said. "The last thing I need is to be the focus of another controversial murder investigation. And if word is already starting to spread around town…"

"So we need to find the root of the source," Brendan said.

"Yes, but who?"

She had no idea who would have stirred up such terrible stories about a man who had recently died. But she thought she did have an idea of who she could talk to that might know where to point them.

"Want to take a ride back out to Coastal Gems?" Marie asked Brendan.

"I do not. I heard what Deputy Miles told you. I don't think that's the best idea."

She was rather embarrassed that she had nearly made such a rash decision. She considered it for a while and then took out her phone. She googled Coastal Gems and pulled up the number.

"Marie, what are you doing?" Brendan asked cautiously.

The phone rang in her ear and was answered right away. "Coastal Gems," said a bright, singsong voice. "This is Gale."

Relieved that it wasn't Rick Minor or any other agent who might have asked for her name, Marie responded, "Gale, it's Marie Fortune. I know it's very short notice and we just spoke last night, but do you think you could give me another five minutes or so?"

There was hesitation from the other end. Marie was also pretty sure she could hear a few people speaking in the background. It sounded very busy in the Coastal Gems offices. "I get a lunch break in half an hour. But I can't risk coming to your house again. Things here are…well, they're *weird* today. How about the pier on West Tide Avenue?"

Marie nearly laughed at the irony of it. Of course Gale would want to meet at the pier on West Tide Avenue—the last place anyone had seen her mother. Well, allegedly, anyway.

"Sure," Marie said, biting back the bitterness and pushing those thoughts away.

"Great. Meet me there in about forty minutes."

Then, without a goodbye, Gale ended the call. "Well," Marie said, looking to Brendan and Posey, "Gale said things are weird over there today. I imagine that means they've caught wind of the rumors about Decker."

131

"Yeah, but Gale already knew," Brendan said. "So I'm sure others knew, too."

"Maybe they just weren't aware of how bad it was."

"Marie...let me try to be the voice of caution here," Brendan said. "If the rumors are getting around, maybe Miles is right. Just lay low."

"I know I should. But...well, I know it sounds dumb but I feel like I'm part of it. I was among the people he tried to bully. He wanted my house and I found him lying in a pool of still-wet blood. Throw in the fact that the cops have me listed as a potential suspect and I can't just sit back and wait."

"Okay then," Brendan said. "Let's go. Where are we meeting her?"

Again, she thought of the location—of the very same pier she'd visited not too long ago to try to commemorate the day she thought her mother had disappeared from the face of the planet. She wondered if this was the universe's way of coming full circle. She wasn't even sure if she believed in such things, but it certainly felt like it.

"You know, I think I'll go this one alone."

"You sure?" Brendan asked. He sounded mildly disappointed, maybe even a little hurt.

"Yeah. In the meantime, if you want something to do while I'm gone, you can snoop around Mr. Winslow's door. See what you can find out about him."

"Um, okay. I mean I could use the EVP recorder and it would likely be able to hear whatever is going on behind that door..."

"Oh my God, Brendan, I was just kidding."

"Oh, see, I didn't get that."

Posey laughed at them as she got to her feet and made her way into the kitchen. She gave Marie a knowing little wink as she made her exit. Marie barely noticed it, though. She was too wrapped up in the second meeting with Gale and the idea of revisiting West Tide Pier and the feeling that even now, her mother—though very likely alive somewhere in the world—was somehow still haunting her.

CHAPTER TWENTY SIX

Now that the facts of her mother's disappearance were very different, revisiting the pier did not feel quite as somber when Marie stepped onto it forty-five minutes later. When she saw Gale sitting on one of the little benches along the side of the pier before it even made it out to the water, she did sense the tension of the situation, though. If she were thinking more rationally, she shouldn't be here. And it had been clear from Gale's tone and hurriedness on the phone that she wasn't totally comfortable with the meeting, either.

Marie sat down next to her. Gulls cried out behind them, swooping just above the surface of the ocean. Before Marie could thank the woman for meeting with her again, Gale started talking. She did so quickly, making it clear without having to say so that she did not intend to stay very long.

"I suppose you wanted to speak because it seems a gossip bomb has gone off," she said.

"That's one way to put it. First of all, I just want you to know that I didn't say a word about what you told me last night. You have my word on that."

"Oh, I know it wasn't you. Before I spoke with you, I had a conversation with Rick."

"Rick Minor?"

"Yes. We had gotten a few inquiries yesterday about Mr. Decker. People that have lived around here a while and have even a passing interest in real estate know that Avery Decker got his start with Coastal Gems—was one of the first agents with the company, as a matter of fact. So I told Rick what I knew, hoping to do some damage control, trying to find out ways to sort of distance ourselves from him just in case it all got out. But Rick flipped his lid. I mean, he went a little nuts. He accused me of talking bad about the man who had trained him, taught him everything he knew. But then he looked into it himself. Looked back through Decker's Coastal Gems records and saw for himself. There are entries in his records with the company that he sort of sniped from us when he went solo—notes on properties he convinced us weren't a good investment and then went and secured for himself. That made Rick angrier than me telling him my theory about Decker and the stigmatized properties."

"Why didn't you tell me you had told Rick when we spoke last night?"

"For the same reason I wish Rick would shut up about this. I didn't want a lot of people to know and thought Rick would help keep it that way. Plus, no offense, with Rick, it was business. And I didn't want to tell you about any sort of controversial information about business at Coastal Gems."

"So do you think it's Rick Minor?" Marie asked. "You think Rick Minor has been telling everyone about what Decker was up to for the last day or so?"

"Oh, I *know* it's him. He told me. And he's been telling people that matter. That's how the news has spread so quickly. He's even reached out to some of Mr. Decker's old clients to make sure they know. I think he means well, wanting to make sure the clients hold no grudges, but…it's getting bad. I already know of at least three families that are irate. I know Rick is trying to save face, trying to make sure Coastal Gems is in the clear for all of this, but I'm afraid it's going to have the opposite effect."

Marie wasn't sure how to feel about this new development. On the one hand, with more people angry about Decker's past dealings, it certainly opened up the pool of potential murder suspects. But on the other hand, she also assumed that the more people learned about him, the more people would hear how his body was discovered—that Marie Fortune, that new lady that moved into her eccentric aunt's old house and tried turning it into a bed-and-breakfast, had been the first on the scene. And that she appeared to have been caught almost red-handed.

"Any chance he'd talk to me?" Marie asked.

"Rick? I have no clue. Up until this morning, he seemed pretty certain it was you that killed Mr. Decker. But now…now I don't know. He's so deep in trying to save the reputation of Coastal Gems that I don't think he'd even think twice about it now."

Now, feeling a more urgent need to make sure her name was cleared, Marie knew she had to take the risk. Yes, Rick Minor had told her that he'd call the cops if she showed up again, but he was actively spreading a story that could potentially make her look even worse. And she was going to have to stop it if she had any hope of getting out of this. She felt somewhat certain her name would be cleared in terms of the murder of Avery Decker. But now she had her already dinged reputation to think about—a reputation that was already in question within this small and tightknit town.

"Are you going to go by and talk to him?" Gale asked.

"I'm going to try," she said, as she got to her feet. And with that, Marie hurried away from the bench, already considering her next move.

***

As soon as Marie stepped through the door at Coastal Gems, she saw that Gale had not been exaggerating. There was another woman sitting at the desk Gale had been occupying yesterday, but Marie barely even saw her. Behind this woman, Rick Minor was pacing the large open space. He had a cell phone tucked between his shoulder and ear, his neck bent awkwardly to hold it. He held a thick binder of residential listings in his hands, flipping through them quickly as he spoke very loudly and exaggerated to the person on the other end of the phone. He looked like he might be working on Wall Street or setting up some important meeting for a senator rather than learning about a recently deceased real estate agent.

"Can I help you?" the sheepish woman at the front desk said.

"I need to speak with Mr. Minor, actually."

"Oh," the woman responded. She then cringed a little as if to say: *Oh, you poor woman.*

Marie waited patiently, though Minor seemed to switch gears completely when he saw her. He said, "Can I call you back later?" to whomever he was speaking to and then tossed the binder on a nearby desk. It gave an impressive slapping sound, quite similar to a gunshot, as it landed.

"What do you want?" he snapped.

"Just a minute of your time," Marie answered.

He was fuming but she could see him showing restraint as he considered something for a moment. "Come on back to my office." His tone of voice was softer now, but Marie thought it might simply be for the benefit of the woman at the front desk.

Marie stepped beyond the front desk and followed Minor to the back of the large room. As she followed him, she was once again struck by the attention to detail, making the interior of Coastal Gems seem like a tidy beachfront home. Minor's office was located in the back left of the place and it was almost like stepping into a study. When she passed through the door, Minor closed it behind her. He didn't bother sitting down before he started talking.

"I told you I'd call the police if you came by here again."

"Maybe that's okay," Marie said. "Listen…no matter what you think of me or what you think I may have done, you've got to know that spilling all of Decker's secrets around town is not only exposing a dead man's dirt, but it also has the potential to make me look very bad."

"So you're not as much worried about what people might think of Decker as you are what they might think of you?"

"If I'm being honest…partly. But you have to think about this, Minor. Why the hell would I want Decker dead? Yes, he sort of bullied me as he tried to get me to think about selling my house. But that's it. If anything, his wanting to buy June Manor makes it seem more valuable to the public eye."

"Does it? You weren't on to what he was doing from that start?"

"No, not from that start. But—full disclosure, here—I was looking into what I thought he might be up to. That's why I was meeting with him. To ask questions. To confront him on it." She paused here and asked: "And why were you there?"

"I was simply going by the place to get a look at it, to see if it would be worth taking on as a Coastal Gems property. We briefly listed it a month or so ago but the Realtor who was in charge let it go for some reason, and that's when Decker apparently snapped it up—but I didn't know that at the time. Yes, I knew the grisly history of the land itself but, as you saw, it's a rather unique property. It was just a coincidence that Decker was there at all."

A little warning bell rang in Marie's head. Was she really supposed to believe that Minor showing up to the property was a coincidence? Especially given his history—both good and bad—with Decker?

"And you had absolutely no idea what he was up to?" Marie asked. "Undercutting all those people? Trying to scare them out of their properties?"

"The first I ever heard of it was when he was pursuing that property in Ogunquit. It seemed smart to me. I had no idea he had been doing the same sort of thing here in Port Bliss. It seemed too…too *mean*."

"And what are you doing now? Reaching out to property owners who purchased through him?"

"Yes," he said, sounding irritated. "I'm just trying to make sure everything is copacetic with those folks. There are more than I imagined, honestly. I've only gotten an earful a few times this morning, but...I have to make sure no one comes after us because of what *he* did and..."

He stopped and sighed here, hands on his hips as he looked accusingly at Marie. "No," he said after several seconds. "No, I can't speak with you about this. Maybe it *wasn't* you, but you were there and I'm sorry...even associating with you because of that could look bad. So once again, I'm going to have to ask you to leave."

Marie's first instinct was to argue against it. But honestly, what was the point? The damage had already been done and given the state of mind Minor was in, any further pleading for him to shut up would only make her look even guiltier. She was going to have to let this play out and hope the police could find the actual killer before it was too late.

Without another word, Marie left Rick Minor's office. She'd made it to the door, her hand pulling it open, when she heard his voice behind her.

"Ms. Fortune, wait a second!"

He looked troubled about something, as if his brain was hung up on a thought that didn't quite make sense. "Yes?" she asked.

"He came to your home...to your great-aunt's house, wanting to buy. Is it in the same state as these other properties we're learning about?"

Marie wasn't quite sure why a smile came to her face. She thought of Brendan and of Boo and for perhaps the first time since officially moving into the house, felt perfectly fine thinking of the place as *her home*.

"You know, I think it was," she answered honestly. "But it's not anymore."

The look on Minor's face as she made her exit was even more confused than it had been moments ago. And though there was a sense of accomplishment and pride to her statement, she found it hard to continue smiling. Because while she was headed back to that place she now thought of as home, she'd be returning with no answers and a very uncertain future.

CHAPTER TWENTY SEVEN

When she arrived back at June Manor, the front door was locked. That meant Posey was gone. She unlocked the door and stepped inside; the place was silent and completely empty. Well, she wasn't sure about the *empty* part. There was no telling what Atticus Winslow might be up to. She had not seen Brendan's car in the driveway, so he was likely somewhere in town—probably trying to conduct his own research into Avery Decker. Or maybe scouring out some of the presumably haunted locations he had been involved in.

Only Boo was there to greet her as she went into the kitchen and poured a cup of coffee from what remained of the mornings pot. She walked out onto the back porch with Boo at her side. She did not stop there, though. She walked out onto the beach, crossing the freshly redesigned walkway Benjamin had built for her, connecting the outer rim of the back yard to the beach.

She found a spot in the sand and sat there, watching the waves crash, the water rolling up and then being sucked back out to sea. She closed her eyes and listened to the ocean, felt the sun on her skin. It was warm, but not hot. And there was a moderate coolness to the sand she had not felt since arriving in Port Bliss. These, she knew, were small hints that summer was coming to a close. And whenever she thought of that, she understood how bad that could be for business. For a bed-and-breakfast in a coastal town, summer should be the busiest months, of course. But the only time she'd ever considered herself *busy* was when some of Brendan's fans had more or less followed him in during those first few days of business.

How does that feel so long ago?

It was a daunting thought, one made even more daunting as she opened her eyes and took in the seemingly endless expanse of the ocean. She breathed deeply of the salt air and then made her way back to the yard. As she crossed it and came to the porch, she looked up and saw a figure standing there. It spooked her at first, but then she recognized the familiar face. Brendan had come back while she had been trying to calm herself on the beach.

"Everything okay?" Brendan asked. "You looked…thoughtful out there."

"How long were you watching?" she asked as she came up the stairs.

"A while. Long enough to be able to tell something is bothering you. Not long enough to be creepy, I promise. So I ask again: everything okay? How'd it go with Gale?"

"Well, the meeting with Gale became a meeting with Rick Minor immediately afterwards." She spent a few minutes telling her all she had learned—about how everyone in town was soon going to know about Decker's schemes because of Minor's misguided attempt at saving the reputation of Coastal Gems.

"So you think your name is going to get butchered right along with Decker's?" he asked.

"Yeah. And I hate to think that way, you know? I mean, a man is dead and here I am all wrapped up in my own reputation and trying to salvage my own business. It's just—"

"Hello?" another voice said from the back door. They both turned and when Marie saw the man standing there, she wasn't sure how to feel. It was Deputy Miles, peeking out. And just as Marie opened her mouth to say hello, she saw another man behind him—Sheriff Jenkins.

"Deputy Miles, hello," Brendan said, doing what he could to break the tension. He stepped forward and shook Miles's hand with a smile. "Good to see you again."

"Likewise," Miles said, though his expression made it clear that he wasn't quite sure why Brendan Peck was once again at June Manor—on the heels of another murder that seemed to involve Marie Fortune, no less.

Marie watched as Brendan then introduced himself to Sheriff Jenkins. She wasn't sure why, but the fact that Jenkins was accompanying Miles made Marie very uneasy. Jenkins wasn't a very intimidating man but in a town like Port Bliss, the title of Sheriff alone was enough to garner a sense of authority and respect.

When introductions were made, Miles gave Jenkins a tiny frown before looking at Brendan. "Mr. Peck, we'd like to have a word in private with Ms. Fortune if you don't mind."

"Of course," he said, and started walking toward the door.

"Actually, it's fine," Marie said. "I'm okay with him being here. I've told him everything that's going on."

Jenkins looked a little troubled by this but gave Miles a shrug. "If you're certain," he said.

"It shouldn't take long anyway," Miles said. I'll make this quite simple and to the point. "Ms. Fortune, I want this to be the absolute last time I have to tell you to leave this case alone. Believe it or not, we, as the Port Bliss and Winscott County police, are perfectly capable of doing our jobs."

"Yes, sir, I know that. But I—"

"Rick Minor has officially filed a complaint against you," Jenkins said. "However, we also aren't blind to the fact that he may be the source of some salacious rumors being passed around about Mr. Decker. These rumors have gotten quite a few property owners up in arms and if it keeps going on this way, this case is going to get ugly. And with you running around conducting your own investigation, it's only going to make matters worse. You can understand that, right?"

"Yes," Marie said. The really lousy part of it was that she *did* understand.

"It's a small town," Miles said. "If word gets around that you're poking your nose into the investigation, it's not going to look good for you. And it's going to be even harder to clear you as a suspect. So please…just let us do our jobs."

"If we have to come out here again and have this talk," Jenkins added, "we'll have to officially press charges. This is your last warning. And I shouldn't even give you this one."

"I understand."

Jenkins and Miles gave them both polite nods. Apparently, Boo didn't understand any of it. He was sniffing at Miles's feet and pawing at his shoes playfully, wanting to be petted. When both officers left through the back door, Boo did not seem very pleased.

Marie stood there, frozen for a moment. She felt like everything was spinning out of control. Yes, she knew very well that her constant interfering in the case could complicate things. But there was a supernatural element to what she was investigating and that was not something the police were going to take seriously.

Only, there's no active supernatural element, some wiser part of her spoke up. *Even if you can prove beyond a shadow of a doubt that Decker was dealing in stigmatized properties, it will do absolutely nothing to clear your name. That's going to be done in a forensics lab and interrogation rooms.*

She ran a hand through her hair in frustration. She felt like crying but wasn't sure why, exactly. Frustration, she supposed.

"Hey…" Brendan said.

"Sorry you had to hear that," she said. "And sorry you're having to see *this*…"

She felt herself cracking a bit, and knew she was going to cry. Not a full-on sob fest, but certainly a few tears. She started for the back door but was stopped when Brendan grabbed her arm. He did it softy, and when she stopped, his hand slid down her forearm and to her hand. Gripping her hand, he turned her around. She looked up at him, hating that he was seeing her like this but also sort of enamored that they were looking at one another eye-to-eye, less than a foot apart.

"If you need to vent, I'm a good listener."

"No thanks. Talking about it is the last thing I need to do right now."

"If you need a hug, I'm okay at that, too," he said with an unsteady grin.

She said nothing, only smiled back and looked away. Apparently, that was answer enough. Brendan pulled her in close and wrapped his arms around her. It was not the soft romantic embrace she had been expecting. He seemed to be making every effort to be a gentleman and not press anything inappropriate together.

When she gave in and rested her head on his shoulder, some of that thin distance evaporated and they were completely together. It felt nice; Marie could not remember the last time she'd been hugged like this.

"You going to be okay?" he asked.

"Yeah. I need to do what they said. Need to stay out of the way."

He nodded and she could feel his slightly stubbly cheek against the side of her brow. She brought her head up, feeling a little too vulnerable in his arms. It was nice and she appreciated it, but she couldn't let herself fall too deeply into it. The last thing she needed right now was to put any sort of focus on the minor crush she had been developing on him.

She pulled back, but not away. This time when their eyes locked, their faces were closer. Marie felt it happening before she even moved—the lure of it, the little spark of energy. And in a span of about three blissful seconds, his eyes got closer, their noses barely grazed one another, and he was kissing her.

Even though she had not been expecting it, she did not pull away. Honestly, she didn't even feel that surprised. If *anything* surprised her, it was how easily and how quickly she was able to fall into it. She felt his hands at her waist and she could sense them wanting to move. But she also got the sense that even though he initiated the kiss, it had taken him by surprise, too.

It was slow and soft, and when they pulled apart about ten seconds later, she felt swimmy-headed. She tried stepping away from him but found she didn't really want to. He did, though. And there was a slightly mortified look on his face.

"I'm so sorry," he said. The redness in his cheeks showed that he meant it.

"It's okay," she said. They were still standing very close to one another. Marie wasn't sure if it was the light-headedness or the fact that she had not felt close to someone in so long, but she found herself reaching for his hand. She took it and met his eyes again. "It's so okay that I think I'd like for you to do it again."

He took her other hand and pressed his forehead to hers. "And I *want* to do it again. But Marie…without giving you a sad story and playing little violins, this is the closest I've gotten to anyone in a very long time—before the kiss, even. And given the partnership we have going on—if you want to even call it that—I don't think it would be smart."

She was both insulted and impressed. She wasn't sure she'd ever had a man be so honest with her before. She sighed and leaned back into him for another hug.

"Rain check?" he asked.

She almost said yes right away. But the idea that his remarks indicated he might also have a past with failed relationships and trust issues made her hesitant. So, instead, she said, "We'll see."

They stayed that way for several seconds, with waves crashing musically behind them. Marie felt like she could have stayed there for the rest of the afternoon. But the distant sound of knocking caused her to break the embrace and look toward the back door.

"Someone knocking at the front?" Brendan asked.

"Sounds like it. One second."

She left him on the patio and when she turned her back to him, she finally allowed a massive smile to cross her face, a direct result of their kiss. It was the best first kiss with a guy she'd ever had. When she walked toward the front door, she felt like she was *floating*.

The knocking came again moments before she reached the door. When she answered it, there was a friendly, familiar face on the other side. And for reasons she could not quite identify in the moment, she wasn't sure if she was happy to see that face or not.

It was Robbie Dunne. He smiled widely at her and she did her best to match it. But before either of them could say anything, she saw Robbie looking through the open doorway, into the sitting room. Marie looked back and saw Brendan at the edge of the dining room entrance. And as she looked from one to the other, the look of disappointment on both their faces was evident.

"Robbie, it's good to see you!" She beamed. "Come on in."

He did, his smile a little dimmer than it had been seconds ago. And when Marie closed the door behind her, she could already feel the tension starting to grow.

CHAPTER TWENTY EIGHT

To his credit, Brendan did his very best not to snoop or spy. He set about making tea, rummaging through the cabinets and putting on the kettle as Marie and Robbie took a seat in the sitting room. Marie really was happy to see Robbie. She hadn't seen him in several weeks and he had been the first familiar face she'd seen when she'd come to Port Bliss—a face that had spent a bit of time bouncing around in her head for those first few weeks if she was being honest with herself.

"Your appearances are getting fewer and further between," Marie said. "Everything been going well?"

"Yes, actually. There have been some huge business decisions in the last few weeks. I've made some trips to Boston to square some things away and the future is looking pretty good. But if I'm interrupting something," he said, his eyes looking quickly in the direction of the kitchen.

"No, not at all," Marie said. "You're perfectly fine. That's Brendan. He's just a friend who's been helping me out with some of the bed-and-breakfast stuff." But even as she told that slightly modified lie, she was thinking about the kiss. "So what's been going on with the restaurant? What big decisions?"

He chuckled and looked at her as if she were trying to play a prank on her. "Are we seriously going to just sidestep the rumors gong around?" he asked. "That's why I'm here, Marie. I heard about your potential involvement in Avery Decker's murder and had to come check in on you. Of course, I don't think you did it, but the rumors are starting to swirl."

"Starting to, or have already made the rounds?"

"Pretty much made the rounds, I guess. The biggest chunk of news is coming from all the bad business practices Decker was pulling off. So I think you might have another day or two before you become the big talking point again."

"That's good…I guess."

Robbie waited a beat and looked around at the quiet sitting room. "Is business doing any better?" he asked.

"Not really. I've got one guest that's here for an indefinite period of time, and then Brendan, who is around for a few days."

"Is he the guy that was here when all the stuff with the hot air balloon death of Alfred Ryker went down?"

"Yeah, that's him."

Robbie seemed slightly troubled by this for a moment but seemed to let the unease roll right off of him. "Still," he said, "it's peaceful here. Quiet. It has a good feel, you know? I really do wish June could see what you've done with the place."

"Sometimes I do, too. But if she ever was able to pop in for a visit, I just hope the place is packed out."

"Does it feel like *your* place yet?" he asked.

It was a good question, and one he might be happy to know had crossed her mind just recently. "You know, it does here and there. I feel secure in calling it *home.*"

As she said this, she caught sight of Brendan in the kitchen. From her angle, she could not see exactly what he was doing, but she heard the door open and then close; he had apparently stepped back out onto the back porch to give them some privacy. And, she hoped, to maybe think about the kiss they'd shared.

"I was in this house a few times when June owned it," Robbie said. "She'd call for a delivery from Red Reef every now and then. Not often, maybe once every few months. I delivered a few of them and she'd invite me in for coffee or tea. And even back then, I loved this room. All the books, all the open space…"

"Oh, this has always been my favorite room, too. Even as a little girl, sitting on the floor and reading or coloring. Or, sometimes, pretending to read or color and just listening to Mom and Aunt June gossip. Sometimes I still get the urge to get down on that rug and stretch out like a little girl with a good book."

"Seems like a perfectly obvious way to revisit your childhood," he said with a laugh. "And also a great way to reconnect with June. I say go for it the next time the urge strikes you. If it keeps you closer to her, what can it hurt?"

Marie smiled, the idea of it warming her heart. Yet at the same time, something Robbie said seemed to trigger something in her head. *If it keeps you closer to her…*

She was not a detective by any means, but the comment somehow ended up pointing toward Avery Decker. Not only him, but Rick Minor as well.

If it keeps you closer...

What if Minor had been more closely associated with Decker than she'd originally thought—maybe even more than Gale had been aware of? He had certainly seemed very eager to cover the rear end of Coastal Gems from Decker's past actions, making sure everyone knew they had severed ties with him long ago. What if news of Decker's shady actions had started circulating even before he'd died? Gale had already said Minor was positioned to take a very large jump at the company. So wouldn't he want any sort of blemishes on the company to go away? Also, what if...

"Marie, you okay?"

"Yeah," she said, though her thoughts were still on the developing theory that was currently occupying her brain. "But you just said something that made me realize..."

"What is it?" Robbie asked.

She suddenly got to her feet, reaching for her phone as she looked at Robbie with a frown on her face. "Robbie, I'm really sorry. But I have a few calls to make...and they're pretty urgent."

"Oh, okay, sure," he said, getting up. She was somewhat relieved to see that he did not look all that disappointed. If anything, he seemed amused at her sudden burst of excitement. "Anything I can do to help?"

"Not really—though something you just said may have given me an idea to get myself out of yet another murder investigation. So you've done enough."

"Happy to help," he said on the way toward the door. "Give me a call sometime, Marie. I'd love to take you to dinner. Or, you know, drop some sort of inadvertent wisdom on you totally out of the blue."

"I'll do that," she said, already pulling up a number on her phone. She gave him a little wave as he closed the door behind him and then placed her call. As the phone started to ring, she knew she was taking a huge gamble.

But the theory she now had seemed resolute. She wasn't even sure how she had missed it in the first place. Minor had also been on the scene when she had found the body; in fact, he'd come in rather conveniently right behind her.

But what if he had gotten there before her? What if Minor was the killer and, upon leaving, took advantage of Marie's sudden arrival?

It made a terrible kind of sense, one that all but locked into place as the phone started to ring in her ear. It was answered quickly by a voice that was becoming very familiar to her.

"Hello?" came the answer.

"Gale, it's Marie again. Sorry…but I have a huge favor to ask. And a question you might not like."

"Okay…"

And then Marie told her what she was thinking, and asked her favor. Her heart was beating fast as the words came out and by the time Gale had heard it all and agreed to help, Marie was now certain she'd not only cleared her name, but likely figured out who the killer was as well.

With that call over, she had one last call to make. And it was going to be the most difficult of all. She took a deep breath, pulled the number up, and called. After a receptionist answered on the second ring, Marie said: "I need to speak with Deputy Miles, please."

CHAPTER TWENTY NINE

Like most good plans, Marie's seemed foolproof until she actually started to act it out. The first step in the plan was to enter the Red Reef Diner at 3:55 in the afternoon. She did that easily enough, but even as she sat down and ordered a hot chocolate, she started to find little cracks and fissures in her plan. But it was too late now. It had all been set into motion and it was too late to back out now.

It was just after four o'clock, Marie sipping on her hot chocolate, when the door opened behind her. A few moments later, a man came to her table and looked down at her. He looked like he did not want to be there at all. But there was also a look of curiosity on his face as he looked down at Marie.

It was Rick Minor, standing by the table and waiting for an invitation to sit down.

A woman stood behind him. This was Gale, looking around the diner with a thin smile. From this point on, Gale was an integral part of the plan. Marie just hoped the woman could keep her cool. She already seemed a little nervous. She was carrying a small laptop case, holding it close to her side.

"Have a seat, Mr. Minor," Marie said.

He accepted the invitation, but he looked skeptical as he slid into the seat. Gale waited a beat and then slid in next to him.

"Gale says you told her you had something important to talk about but wouldn't tell her what it was," Minor said. "So please, let's just get to it. Please don't take this the wrong way, but I'm not particularly comfortable being around you."

"That's a little unfair," Marie said. "But I suppose I understand. And yes…I wanted to talk to you because this whole thing with Decker has me shaken. It made me wonder why he'd come to me, asking to buy the house when he knew I had turned it into a bed-and-breakfast. I don't know if you're aware of it or not, Mr. Minor, but the house was given to me by my Great-Aunt June. I accepted the gift right away because I've always loved the house. I didn't even get an appraisal on the property. But then I figured Decker must have been interested for a reason, you know? So I looked into it and got an estimated property value for the house and the beach front land. It's more than I would have imagined and, quite frankly, more than I can walk away from. In other words...I'd like to sell the property. And I figured it's the least I could do to bring it to you, since it seems you're having some trouble with Decker having passed away."

As she made her way through it all, she watched the expression on his face change from something close to disgust to what was now the look of a man who had found a winning lottery ticket. But slowly, a look of suspicion bloomed on his face, replacing it.

"Well, given the nature of what I've learned about Decker and most of his dealings, my first question would be: *Why did he want it?* What's wrong with the property, Ms. Fortune?"

She felt another crack forming in her plan. With an enormous payday looming in his future, Marie had been *sure* he'd spring for the bait. But he was either being very cautious, or he really had no idea about her property's history.

"I've wondered that myself," she said, trying to play it out. "You mean to tell me you never heard anything from him about the house before he went his own way? According to Decker himself, he talked to my Aunt June, trying to get the property."

Minor seemed to think hard about it for a moment before shaking his head. He looked almost disgusted that he was even in this situation. "Forget it," he said. "I'm not interested in any property Decker had been trying to purchase in these last few months, so I'm going to pass. And if you're smart, you won't ask another Coastal Gems agent, either."

"Fine with me," Marie said. "Based on the price I got from the estimation and Decker's interest, I'm sure I won't have an issue finding someone to take on the sale."

Minor seemed to have a very hard time getting up from his seat. She could see him debating whether or not to pass up such an opportunity. In the end, though, he was successful. He started to get up from the table but before he did, Marie fired off the last shot she had. And it was a doozy.

"Might want to reconsider this, Mr. Minor," she said very softly. "I mean, come on. I'm not stupid."

"What do you mean?" he hissed.

She leaned closer to him and gave him a stern look. "Mr. Minor...I know it was you. I know you're the one that killed him."

The look that came over his face was one of pure shock and anger. She probably wouldn't have gotten as strong of a reaction if she'd reached across the table and slapped him in the face.

"I did no such thing," he said through clenched teeth. "And how *dare* you even accuse me of such a thing!"

"Rick..." Gale said, opening her laptop bag. She took out a single folder and pushed it over toward him. "We know it was you. Look...right there. I think maybe you've been trying so hard to distance yourself from him after his death because you were helping him."

"I was...I was...*what?*"

"It's right here, Rick," Gale said. "Two of the last three sales he tried to make with Costal Gems were for stigmatized properties. And while he may not have wrapped those sales up...these contracts both have your signature as the broker. And so do the disclosures."

He stared at the folder as Gale opened it, flipped through a few pages, and then tapped at his signature.

"So what? I took advantage of his terrible personality and wrapped up some sales he couldn't. That's smart business."

"But is that why he maybe left?" Marie suggested. "Squabbles between the two of you? Were you catching on to his game, trying to push your way into those stigmatized properties? Maybe working alongside him for a while, you had a list of those properties saved up."

"You knew what he was up to the whole time," Gale said. "And you killed him to cut him out of the picture—so you could pick up where he left off. Just not as an independent, but as part of Coastal Gems. So you could eventually run the place, right? All of those sales would surely put you in the perfect spot for that promotion you've been working for over the past few years."

"This is insane," Minor said. And then, as if he felt the need to defend himself, he leaned across the table, staring straight at Marie. "Of course I knew your house was a mess! Supposedly haunted or some nonsense. I would have surely swooped in and bought it once you went to jail for Decker's murder. And that *will* happen—your arrest *and* my eventual purchase of the property. Once you're behind bars, what choice will you have? And let's be real...*both of you.* This—this garbage you're throwing at me is weak. And you have absolutely no proof..."

Marie cringed. It wasn't a confession by any means, but it might be enough for the next step of the plan to work itself out. Sure enough, seconds after Minor got all of this out, the man sitting in the booth behind her got to his feet. He turned around and greeted the three of them with a confident smile.

It was the first time in several days that Marie was actually happy to see Deputy Miles.

"Mr. Minor, I couldn't help but overhear some pretty interesting details," he said. "Not quite enough for an arrest certainly, but enough to bring you in for questioning and to take a look at some of the paperwork from sales conducted at Coastal Gems over the years. So I'm going to need you to come with me. I'd appreciate it if you'd do it quietly and friendly. I don't *want* to get loud and break out my handcuffs, but I will if I have to."

"But Deputy, you heard all of that out of context and—"

"Maybe so. But I heard enough to make me suspicious, and that's enough for now. So it's your call, Mr. Minor. We can be friendly getting out of here, or we can make a scene."

Marie was curious as to how Minor would handle this. When she'd first seen him upon discovering Decker's body, he'd seemed meek and mild. But when she'd later seen him on the phone with Decker's clients, pacing back and forth in the office, he'd seemed like a bomb about to explode. She watched his face and thought he saw the answer coming.

"How dare you even accuse me of such a thing," he hissed through clenched teeth. He then slammed his hand down on the table, making Marie's hot chocolate jump, sending some sloshing out over the side. "There is not a speck of evidence and I had no reason whatsoever to—"

As his voice got louder and drew the attention of several diners, Miles acted quickly. He stepped behind Minor and tugged his right arm back behind him. He did it quickly and almost casually so that there was no apparently violent action.

Only, Minor wasn't on board that same train. He wheeled away from Miles and gave the deputy a shove. The collective gasp within Red Reef Diner made it seem like all of the sound had been sucked out of the word. That action had basically sealed the deal—and, as far as Marie was concerned, proved his guilt.

151

Miles simply nodded and then, in an act very fast—a little too fast, Marie thought—he grabbed Rick Minor, spun him around, and pushed him into Marie's table. With Minor nearly bent in half, Miles this time yanked his arms back painfully. Minor screamed out as Miles cuffed him.

"Sorry, folks," Minor said. "Go on and finish your lunches."

He then started to lead Minor out of the diner, toward the front door.

"No, no, look, I overreacted," Minor said as they neared the door. "There's no need for this! Come on, you really think I'm the one that killed him? Look, I don't even—"

But by then, he was out the door, led away by Miles. Slowly, the natural noise of the diner picked back up. Even Marie and Gale looked shocked, though they'd had an idea of how it would all play out. Marie let out a shaky sigh of relief and picked her hot chocolate back up, trying her best to transition back into some semblance of normal. Gale, still sitting across from her, looked absolutely horrified. It looked like she might start crying at any moment.

"Oh my God, it was really him," Gale said.

"Seems that way," Marie said, still trying to process the situation. "Are you okay, Gale?"

"Yeah," she said, sliding the files back into her bag. "Just...like you, I guess. Processing it all. I mean, Rick was always a little odd, you know? But I didn't honestly think he'd do something like that...even after you called and told me your theory."

Marie still felt some of the eyes of the Red Reef Diner patrons looking her way. She picked up her hot chocolate and sipped from it. "Thanks for coming out," Marie told Gale. "But I need to get out of here. Too many eyes..."

"Oh, no, I get it. Let's go."

Marie paid for her hot chocolate and as she got up from her table, she peered through the slatted wall and into the bit of kitchen she could see from the counter. She did not expect to see Robbie back there so she was not disappointed when she didn't spot him.

She and Gale parted ways as they left the diner. As Marie walked the familiar course back to her house, she wondered how poor Gale was going to handle things at work now. More than that, given the history around Decker that people were learning about, how would another blemish on the company affect business?

She had nearly reached her driveway when her cell phone rang. The number was listed as coming from Richmond, Virginia. Coming from so far away, she assumed (or, rather, *hoped*) it would be a future guest at June Manor. She answered it and put on her best professional voice. It was harder to find than usual, given what she'd just witnessed at Red Reef Diner.

"This is Marie at June Manor. How can I help you?"

"Hello," a female voice said. "Is this Marie Fortune?"

"It is."

"Thank goodness." The woman's voice was thick and rather pretty, sprinkled with a southern accent. "My name is Theresa Cunningham. I'm having a bit of a problem at my hotel here in town and was hoping you could help me."

"A hotel in Richmond? I'm sorry…I don't think I understand."

But as soon as she got the comment out, she *did* understand. And what Theresa Cunningham said next confirmed it.

"I'm friends with Wallace Jackson—online only, though, I'm afraid. He told me what you did for him at his house and I thought I'd give you a try. I'm sort of desperate. I know you're in Maine…but I'll pay for travel expenses if you could make it down."

And even though she knew she could not travel out of Port Bliss right away—not until the Avery Decker case was closed—Marie answered in a way that was becoming far too easy lately.

"I might just be able to do that," she said. "Can you tell me a bit about what's happening?"

And just like that, Marie started walking up her driveway, listening to ghost stories from a woman more than six hundred miles away.

CHAPTER THIRTY

When Marie walked through the front door, saving Theresa Cunningham's information to her phone, she heard Posey cursing quite loudly in the sitting room. Marie hurried into the room and found her sitting in one of the chairs, looking at her cell phone. Brendan was standing beside her, doing what he could to calm her down.

"Posey, what is it?" Marie asked.

"This damned town! That's what it is! I just don't understand people sometimes…"

Rather than keep asking questions, Marie went over to the chair and tried to get a look at what Posey had up on her phone. Posey handed the phone to her and as Marie looked at the screen, her heart dropped in her chest. There was an ad, prominently placed on Facebook, for a new local business. Not just any business, though—a bed-and-breakfast. The ad read:

Introducing the Newest Bed-and-breakfast to Port Bliss
Shoreline Oaks
Coastal Comforts, Oceanfront Views, the Time of Your Life!
And unlike our competitors…no drama, no ghosts, no problem!

"That's…well, that's very specific now, isn't it?" Marie said.

"And a little mean," Brendan added.

"It is!" Posey agreed, getting to her feet. "I mean, of course there are going to be businesses competing with one another. But I'd say that's borderline slander! They called you out without *really* calling you out."

"She's been pretty upset about it since she saw it ten minutes ago," Brendan said.

"Of course I have! I mean…the nerve!"

"It's okay, Posey," Marie said, though she felt anger rising up in her, too. "After all, it's not like they are being dishonest."

"You wait until I find out who posted this…"

"Find out, and let me know," Marie said. "I'll go have a reasonable and civil discussion with her."

"Yeah, you look into that," Posey said with a huff. "Meanwhile, I'll be in town, trying to figure out who's in charge of this Shoreline Oaks garbage!"

"But Posey..."

Posey shook her head, gave Marie a little sympathetic pat on the shoulder, and headed out the front door. She shut the door a little too hard on her way out for Marie's liking.

"So..." Brendan said, anxious to switch topics. "How'd it go? Did your plan work?"

"I'd say so. Gale had some pretty damning evidence that Rick Minor was in cahoots with Decker. Minor had some surly things to say about it and Deputy Miles was right there to hear it all. I got to watch Miles escort Minor out of the diner after a little outburst."

"That sounds exciting," Brendan said. "Not sure if it's exciting enough for me to overlook the fact that you just used the words *cahoots* and *surly* in less than ten seconds, though."

She gave him a very sarcastic laugh, though she had actually found it funny. "Oh, also, on the way back home, I got a phone call from someone in Richmond, Virginia. A ghost-cleaning sort of thing from the sounds of it."

"Whoa, seriously? When?"

"I scheduled it for next week, hoping this Avery Decker nightmare will all be over by then."

"That's great! Forgive me for being nosy, but is the pay worth the trip down there?"

She shrugged. "I don't even know what to charge for this sort of thing. I felt awful taking that twenty grand from Mrs. Clark. Mr. Jackson's was less than that, but I felt it was still too much."

"If it makes you feel any better, I can tell you with absolute certainty that total frauds charge upwards of twenty thousand for what you're doing. Even more out west—we're talking fifty or sixty grand at times."

"Well, I didn't charge nearly that much for going to Richmond. But yes...I'd consider it a very nice payday."

"And you know, it's an odd profession, but if it's something you want to pursue, I've got at least four names I can give you right now that would be happy to hire you. They're sort of scattered all over the country, though. And I know you've got the B&B to think of."

"I do," she said, glancing around at the sitting room.

"And apparently a guest who has locked himself in his room for an undisclosed period of time."

"Yeah...hey, you know lots of weird folks. Are you absolutely certain the name Atticus Winslow doesn't ring any bells?"

He thought about it for a moment and then shook his head. "Can't say that it does. And speaking of uncertainty..."

"Terrible transition."

"I know. All the same—what do we do about that kiss? Ignore it? Pretend it never happened?"

"That ball is in your court," she said, searching his eyes. "It was nice and I enjoyed it. But you seemed apologetic and I don't know why. I guess it just shows that we don't know each other well enough to quite go there."

"Maybe. But on the other hand, I really want to do it again."

He leaned in and she followed his lead. However, when their faces were about three inches apart, Marie shook her head. It hurt her heart to do so, but she felt it was the right thing to do in the moment.

"I do, too," she whispered, fighting the urge to continue leaning in. "But with everything going on, it seems like just one more thing I could potentially mess up."

He nodded, took a deep, steadying breath, and then took a step away from her. "Business partners for now?"

"I don't know. I've committed to this one in Richmond but after that—I'm not sure. June Manor needs to be my main priority."

"Well, give it some thought. At the risk of sounding selfish, I think it's an opportunity that could work out well for both of us. But for now, I need to go ahead and check out. I was going to wait and stay one more night, but if I leave right now, I can be in Boston before dark. There's a panel I'm on in two days, and I always like to get to a city a day or so early to familiarize myself with haunted landmarks. Makes me seem like I know what I'm talking about when I get there."

"I see," she said. "Are you sure this has nothing to do with the tension that's between us now?"

"Oh, it's that, too. No need to lie about it. But can I give you a call after the panel? I want to stay in touch—maybe find a way to see each other more."

"Yeah, I'd like that."

He stood there, still very close to her, for a few more seconds. It seemed to take a great deal of effort for him to turn away and head up the stairs. She made herself *not* watch him go because she felt it might be a little too cheesy. Instead, she went to the desk and went through the process of checking him out.

When she was done, she pulled out her cell phone and went to her Facebook page. She found the ad for Shoreline Oaks and read over it again. And yes, it did make her angry. Not only was it insulting, but it just added one more thing to her list of worries.

Brendan came back down the stairs just a few minutes later. He handed her the key to his room and started for the door. "Thanks for the room," he said. "This really is a very special place, Marie. Hidden rooms and all."

"Yeah, it sort of is."

She walked him out to the porch. Boo came out of hiding to also follow along, apparently wanting to see his friend off, too. When they were on the porch, Brendan turned to her as he reached the stairs. He was about to say something, but she felt some sort of pull, a longing and excitement she had not been expecting. Despite what she'd said just five minutes ago, she found herself taking advantage of the moment and kissed him before he could say anything. This one was brief, yet equally sweet. When she pulled away, she caught the traces of a dreamlike smile on his face.

"Is that like an incentive to come back?" he asked. "Because if so, it wasn't necessary. It was a nice perk, for sure, though."

She smiled at him and they exchanged a hug that, to her, felt a bit different than the other few they'd shared. It was warmer, more intimate—like they were hiding a secret between them. Which, she supposed, they were. Even Boo stepped away to give them a bit of privacy.

She watched him get into his car, waving him off. As he backed out, he had to stop as another car turned into the driveway. It was not a car she was familiar with; the only ones she knew by sight were Posey's car and Benjamin's beat up work truck. Brendan had to expertly creep all the way to the side of the driveway to allow the car through. It passed by him and he then made his way back out to the road. He gave a little toot of his horn as he disappeared from view.

Seconds later, the new car pulled up beside Marie's car. The glare of the sun on the windshield made it hard for her to see who was driving. But when the door opened and the driver stepped out, Marie was surprised to see Gale standing there.

"Hey, Marie," she said, approaching the porch.

Curious, Boo went down to sniff Gale, and then her car. He wagged his tail at the presence of new scents.

"Hey. Everything okay?"

"Yeah, all is well. News of what happened to Rick is making its way across the Coastal Gems network, so that's fun. But putting that aside, I was wondering if you might have a chance to talk for a bit. Maybe tell me more about the house?"

It seemed like a strange request, but she supposed Gale was just being curious about the house that had brought Avery Decker knocking. Maybe she was trying to make her own sense out of what had happened. If so, Marie could certainly sympathize.

"Yeah, that's fine," Marie said. "If you can hang around awhile, you might even catch dinner."

"That might be doable. Thanks!"

Marie escorted her inside, stepping aside. She whistled for Boo and patted at her legs, but he was too interested in smelling and then urinating on Gale's back tires.

It wasn't until she allowed Gale inside that she realized how strange it was that Gale had come by so soon after Minor had been taken in by the police. What did she have to talk about that had occurred between then and now? And why was she starting to get an unsettled feeling in her gut as Gale walked through the front door?

She didn't know—but it was a question that sat heavily on her mind as she shut the door behind them.

Marie offered Gale one of the seats in the sitting room and she accepted right away. Still, even before her butt was on the cushion, she said: "You know, I'm afraid you may not like me very much when I tell you my reason for coming by."

"I'm not quite sure how to take that," Marie said. She had been in the midst of sitting down herself, but the comment kept her on her feet. "Are you sure everything is okay?"

"Yes. I'm just having a hard time with this...of trying to take advantage of a very unfortunate situation."

"I still don't follow you."

"I went back to the office after we left the diner," Gale said. "I had a look at the records and property history for this house. Do you have any idea what it was last valued at, just before your great-aunt passed away?"

"No. I never cared to sell it, so I didn't bother."

"Well, it's a lot. And I assume Avery Decker knew this. I also assume Rick knew it. After I found his signatures on some of those Decker disclosures, I was *sure* he would jump at the chance to take this house. Look...stigmatized or haunted or creepy or whatever...it's a stunning property. And the improvements you've been making here and there are only adding to it."

She stopped, letting it all settle in. Marie chose her words very carefully when she finally replied: "It almost sounds like you're trying to talk me into selling it."

"Oh, I am. Again, I know it's awful to try to swipe in when Decker is dead and Rick is otherwise occupied. But I don't see why people like Rick should always get the promotions and the paydays. If I could land this house, I could—"

"I'm sorry, Gale, but this house is not for sale. I don't think it ever will be."

Gale nodded, but it was clear that she was very frustrated. In fact, a little flicker of annoyance passed across her eyes for a moment. "You're certain of that? Even if you ever move out from under this shadow of the creepy place by the beach that is supposedly haunted? You'd keep it even then?"

"This house was a gift from my great-aunt, whom I loved very much," Marie said. "No, I will not sell it."

Gale nodded again, this time standing up. She walked almost curiously over to the bookcase and sighed. The sigh seemed forced, though. Her posture was very rigid, her shoulders tight. "Okay," she said. "But please, if you ever do change your mind, don't let this whole Decker and Minor ordeal sour your impression of Coastal Gems. And whatever you do, if Rick Minor happens to still be working with us— which I seriously doubt—make sure he stays far away from it."

Marie was so eager for the woman to leave that she almost missed her last comment.

Almost.

And then a funny thought struck her. It sure seemed convenient that Gale just happened to know about those disclosure forms signed by

159

Minor. Had she made a point to hold on to them? Had she always known about his part in all of it...and planned to use it against him one day?

Plus, the comment she just made indicated that there had been something of a playful nature to it all—as if she had enjoyed the set-up of it all a little too much. It made her eagerness to share information about Minor and Decker all the more convenient and...

"It wasn't Rick Minor at all, was it?" she asked, her heart starting to hammer harder in her chest. "It was...it was *you*."

"Damn," Gale said. She was looking directly at Marie, her little nose scrunched up in a way that would have been cute any other time. She was running her hands along the bookshelf, slowly coming closer to Marie. "I should have left earlier. I really didn't think you'd figure it out."

Marie wasn't sure how to react. Her brain was racing and she felt her adrenaline spike. She supposed it was the appropriate reaction to realizing that she was being stared down by a killer.

CHAPTER THIRTY ONE

The two women simply stared at one another. Marie figured her silence was enough of an answer for Gale. Yes, she had figured it out—that she, Gale, was the killer. And she had no idea how to react to such a revelation. There was a guilty smirk on Gale's face as she continued to walk along the bookcase, now only a few feet away from Marie.

"It was you?" Marie asked. She wanted to tell herself it made no sense, but the more she examined the pieces, it actually *did.* "Did you actually *fake* the signatures on the disclosures?"

"Nope. That was Rick, all the way. He wasn't quite as crooked as Avery, but he wanted to be the top dog so badly that he was willing to help Avery ascend the ladder. Modeled himself after him and everything. So no, those signatures on the disclosures were legit. I started looking for that sort of thing when it became obvious to some people within Costal Gems what Decker was up to, off on his own. He was buying up stigmatized properties, creepy places with wretched histories. Some of them knew after the fact that he'd started doing that at Coastal Gems. But I seemed to be the only one that cared how it might look on the company."

"So you *killed* him?"

"Oh, it seems extreme, I know. But my God, that man was a nightmare. Rick was worse than Decker; I think he may have actually been the one to convince Decker to go solo, hoping he could reap the benefits. And let me tell you…when I heard that you had arrived at that stupid house before Rick did, I could have killed *you*! He was supposed to be the one to find the body. If you hadn't shown up, this would have been so much easier. And not just for me! But I guess in the end, it worked out just like it should have."

Marie felt fear churning like static through her, but she knew she had to stay calm and collected. Posey had gone into town, and Brendan had just left. She was here all alone with Gale. On the other hand, she also sensed that Gale was proud that she'd managed to get this far; maybe if she could get Gale to talk some more she'd show more of her hand—helping to not only free Marie from suspicion, but to bring

161

Avery Decker's real killer to justice. And maybe she'd talk long enough for Posey to make it back in time to help.

"You did this just for...a promotion?" she asked.

"Partly," Gale said with a shrug. "But also because Avery Decker was just a brute. Thought he was God's gift to everything. Ripping off all those clients was only part of it. Do you have any idea how many times he'd call me *sugar* and give me that creepy wink of his? How many times he suggested I'd make it farther if I dressed more provocatively? Or to put just a little meat on my skinny bones? The way I see it is that if I hadn't killed him, someone else was *sure* to do it."

"But there's no proof. If there wasn't enough to convict *me* when I was right there, standing over the body, they won't be able to pin it on Rick, either."

"Not until I call them tomorrow, letting them know about the threatening letter I found in the back of Rick's appointment book."

"What letter?"

Gale smiled. "I don't know yet. Certainly, it'll be from Decker. But how mean do you think I should make it sound?" She paused here, her face taking on a disappointed look as she saw Marie's shock. "Oh, don't be like that," she said. "Marie, I was really hoping you'd just keep this quiet—just between us."

"I don't—"

There was a scratching at the front door, followed by one of Boo's little whines. It made Marie jump at first but she then walked toward the door to let him in. As she did, she crossed right in front of Gale. The two women's eyes were locked but even then, Gale managed to get the jump on her.

Her trailing of the bookcase had brought her to the end of it, just by the entryway. As Marie passed by her, Gale grabbed the small blue vase, holding several fake wildflowers, and brought it sailing through the air in her fist.

Marie cried out and managed to jump back at just the last moment. The plastic petal of one of the flowers literally brushed the tip of her nose. Right away, though, Gale tossed the vase at her. It struck Marie in the shoulder, sending a little flare of pain down her arm. And then Gale came rushing at her.

As Boo started to bark and pound against the door outside, aware of his owner's peril, Marie tried to fully comprehend what, exactly, was

162

happening. This mousy little woman—who somehow was also a killer—was charging her as if they were playing football. Marie's first reaction was to dodge and run. She'd only been in one fight in her life, a second grade scuffle over a Trapper Keeper on the playground. But on the other hand, Gale was frail-looking and small. She could probably take her down pretty easily, and wouldn't that be very convenient after she called the police to tell them she had Decker's killer right there in the manor?

At the last moment, Marie opened her arms to catch Gale in an improvised hold. Instead, though, Gale slammed her shoulder into Marie's chest. The force of the impact took her by immediate surprise and sent her back against one of the sitting room chairs. As that pain went spiraling through her body, Gale swung the vase again. Marie, still stumbling from the chair, managed to get her arm up before the vase smashed into the side of her face. The vase did not break, though she heard the glass cracking. Marie finally lost her balance, her right leg caught on the chair. She went down to the floor hard. Outside, it sounded like Boo was doing his best to jump through the door, snarling and scratching and thumping.

Gale stood over Marie, that same innocent-looking smile on her face. Marie backed up, using her hands to slide herself backward, but she met the wall sooner than she expected.

"Maybe I can find some way to pin your murder on someone else, too," Gale said as she raised the vase, the flower finally slipping out. "Wasn't there some other woman from Coastal Gems that came by when you first moved in? Maybe I—"

She was interrupted by a strange sound—something almost like a bell, only hollower. From the floor, Marie watched as Gale's eyes fluttered closed and her knees went out. As she collapsed to the floor, falling just inches away from Marie, the source of that odd sound was revealed.

Atticus Winslow stood there, holding a large frying pan in his hand. He stared at Gale's body with a strange look and then at the frying pan. "Hope you don't mind, I nicked it from the kitchen when I heard the commotion," he said.

"Of...of course," Marie said. "Thank you so much..."

She slowly got to her feet, looking down at Gale. She was moving her hands reflexively and letting out a little moan.

"What was all the fuss about?" Atticus asked.

"She came to talk about maybe buying the house and…well, she murdered a man recently and…it's a very long story."

"Oh," Atticus said. "Well then…I came down for tea. Mind if I put a kettle on?"

Marie was bewildered, adrenaline and fear still coursing through her. She only gave a nod, and Atticus headed toward the dining room at once. He carried the frying pan with him.

As Marie fumbled into her pocket for her phone to call the police, Boo continued to scratch at the door. She hurried over and let him in. He blasted inside, barking and looking frantically around. When he saw Gale, he came to a skidding stop and calmed at once. He sniffed at her for a bit and then came to Marie's side. He whined, looking up at her for confirmation that she was okay.

She patted him on the head and said: "I'm okay, boy."

He seemed fine with this and then went sniffing around the sitting room, perhaps looking for any other signs of danger. And even though there were clearly none there, Marie appreciated it. Because if this house had proven anything to her, it was that nothing was ever as it seemed.

She was slowly getting used to it and that, perhaps, was the scariest thing of all.

CHAPTER THIRTY TWO

Marie watched as Sheriff Jenkins escorted Gale through the front door and to a waiting patrol car out in the driveway. There was another officer down there, waiting. Marie knew his face but not his name. But at this rate, she assumed she'd know every single member of the Port Bliss police force within another few months.

As Jenkins led Gale out, Deputy Miles hung back in the sitting room. He was looking around with a perplexed look on his face, his eyes finally settling on Marie. She was sitting in one of the chairs, drinking lavender tea Posey had brewed to help calm her nerves.

"That left wrist looks a little swollen," Miles pointed out. "That the one you used to block the second blow?"

"Yeah."

"I'm no doctor, but you might want to get that checked out."

"I will. I'm still a little too jittery to drive."

"Speaking of which, this thing with Gale is still no slam dunk. But if everything you said she told you checks out, it'll be close. Given that, and the total lack of evidence against you other than two strands of hair, you're free to leave town if needed."

"She mentioned planting some sort of a note in Minor's appointment book, to be written out from Decker. I don't know if that helps at all."

"It certainly doesn't hurt."

"So I'm no longer a suspect, right?"

"That's right," he said, heading for the door. "But I do have to say…you have the absolute worst luck about being in the wrong place at the wrong time."

"Don't I know it."

Miles gave her a smile and a tip of his hat before walking out. Boo followed him, making sure he made it to the door.

Marie got to her feet, intending to head to the kitchen to get some ice for her wrist. She figured she'd be okay to drive to the doctor, though it was past five and she didn't feel like driving an hour to the nearest hospital. Yet as she got to her feet, an unexpected figure appeared from the dining room.

It was Atticus Winslow, and he appeared as if from nowhere. Remarkably, he had a Ziploc bag filled with ice in his hand. He crossed the sitting room and handed it to her without a word.

"Thank you," she said. "Sorry if there was too much commotion. But it was…well, it was a very unexpected situation."

"Yes, I gathered as much."

He stood there awkwardly as she applied the ice pack to her wrist and sat back down. Boo entered the room and slowly approached Winslow. The man eyed Boo skeptically but held his ground.

"Mr. Winslow, can I ask you one question?" she asked.

"If you must," he said. His face showed an expression of irritability, but she sensed that the annoyed tone in his voice was something of an act.

"What brings you to Port Bliss? I only ask because I've only once seen you leave the house. And your saving me just now was the most active I've seen you."

He sighed deeply and frowned. For a moment, Marie thought she might have somehow insulted him. He was definitely a tough character to read.

"Personal matters," he answered at last. And with that, he started walking away, toward the staircase.

"Thanks again for the ice. And potentially saving my life."

He only gave a nod at first, but then, when he got to the stairs he paused and looked back at her. "If you don't mind, I think I may require another few days here. A week at least."

"Absolutely. We can do that."

"And…what's the schedule for dinner? Is it every night?"

"If Posey—my cook—is told there is a need for it, she is happy to whip something up."

"Hmmm."

It was the last thing he said before he started making his way up the stairs. Boo watched him go, walking to the entryway. When Winslow was out of sight, Boo turned back to Marie. If there was any way for a dog to look confounded, it was on Boo's face when he looked at her.

"Don't ask me," Marie said.

She held the ice on her wrist, looking toward the stairs. How had Winslow known she had hurt her wrist? How had he known she was going to get ice? She figured if Brendan was there with her, he'd be happy to share some spooky theories about it all.

But with Gale having attacked her and then arrested, the house had fallen into silence again. And a spooky theory was the absolute last thing she needed.

CHAPTER THIRTY THREE

As Marie read about the charges against Gale in the local paper, she also caught a glimpse of a familiar ad, this time in newsprint rather than digital form. And it took up half of page four. It was that same ad from Shoreline Oaks. She read it and tossed the newspaper into the recycling bin in the kitchen. Still, the text remained, plastered in her head: *And unlike our competitors…no drama, no ghosts, no problem!*

Yes, it was irritating, but she could not complain—not yet, anyway. Three days had passed since Sheriff Jenkins had taken Gale out of June Manor in handcuffs. In that time, she had booked three guests, one of whom had checked in earlier that morning and had taken the one guest room downstairs. Atticus Winslow, of course, was still in his room for at least another four days, and the other new guest was due to arrive next week. That, in addition to the few guests booked for the end of October (dedicated fans of the supernatural who had come to June Manor during Brendan's first run) had her looking toward the future with something very close to hope.

Of course, there was also the trip to Richmond. She was due to leave tomorrow and had already started packing. She couldn't believe she was actually going to do it. She and Boo, on a twelve-hour drive to Virginia. She'd already been paid a deposit on her services, so it wasn't like she could back out anyway.

She wished Brendan could be part of the trip. It would ease her mind and obviously give them ample time to connect. But she had only received a single text from him since he'd left, just to let her know that a few people at the panel he'd been on had asked about the Ghostly Grounds—the moniker many in paranormal circles were using to refer to June Manor.

All of this raced through her mind as she stood in front of the hidden room in the furthest of the upstairs bedrooms. She'd come to the room several times in the last few days, often not even fully aware she was heading there until she opened the closet to reveal the hidden room. But she did not step inside it; she wasn't necessarily scared of the room, but she knew if she stepped in and looked at the book, the postcards, and the letters, she'd become obsessed. Her gut told her that based on what she'd found in that book, her mother was alive. And if she gave herself over to that, it would consume her.

Also, if she was being honest with herself, the book sort of freaked her out. Even looking at it from the doorway set her on edge. On a few occasions, Boo had followed her to the bedroom but when she opened the door, he would back away. His usually inquisitive nose seemed to want nothing to do with Aunt June's hidden room.

That should be your first warning sign, she told herself as she stood in the doorway.

She was looking into the room, thinking about her trip to Richmond, when someone knocked on the bedroom door behind her. She turned, expecting to see Posey, but was surprised to find Robbie Dunne.

For a moment, Marie felt like she had been caught doing something she shouldn't. But as that fleeting thought passed by, she realized that it came from someone else knowing her secret—knowing about the hidden room.

"Hey," Robbie said. "Posey said she thought you were up here. Is it okay that I came up? You look…startled."

"No, it's perfectly fine. In fact…you knew Aunt June well enough so maybe you'd find this interesting, too."

She stepped aside and waved him into the closet. When he joined her, he looked into the room and gave her a puzzled look. "What, exactly, am I looking at?"

"One of Aunt June's many secrets."

She then told him all about Benjamin discovering the room and the things she'd found in it. As she spoke, Robbie looked like he wanted to go inside but, because Marie was keeping her distance from it, he did the same. Oddly enough, as she explained the entire situation to him, she found that it actually helped to verbalize it all to someone who wasn't particularly close to the house. It made her feel a little less crazy.

"Hold on," Robbie said. "So you mean to tell me you found a postcard from your mom to June from eleven years ago?"

"Yes."

"So that's incredible, right? That means there's a good chance she's still alive today, too."

"I try to see it like that, but it starts to feel more like I've just been lied to by everyone I ever really trusted."

"Oh, yeah, I suppose I could see that, too." He cleared his throat awkwardly and pointed to the book, still not walking into the room. She supposed he was doing it out of respect. "So what's the book about?"

"Oh, that's another oddity, too. It's about séances and ghosts. Borderline occult stuff."

"June was into that stuff?"

"Apparently. Which was news to me."

"Huh," was all Robbie had to say. Then, speaking slowly as if he was selecting each word very carefully, he asked: "And are you into that stuff? I know the first few weeks here at the manor might have almost forced you to."

"I honestly don't know," she said. She then wondered what Robbie might say about the reason behind her trip to Richmond and bit back a smile.

"Well, forgive me if this is being too forward," Robbie said, "but what about psychics? Do you buy into any of that?"

"I don't know. Never really even thought about it. Why do you ask?"

He sighed and rolled his eyes. "Okay, bear with me. There's a woman who works as a cook down at the diner. She's in her fifties and isn't really into spooky stuff, but does buy into a lot of New Age teachings. Crystals, restorative healing, things like that. Her daughter is a self-proclaimed psychic. And while I don't personally buy into it, I know of two different people who have visited her and got freaked out about what she was able to tell them. And her mother *swears* it's legit."

"And why are you telling me this?"

"Because if she can do the sorts of things they say she can, she might be able to offer you some insight into your mom."

"Oh, I don't know about that," she said. Yet even as she said it, she had to cross her arms to ward off the little chill that raced through her.

"Just something to think about. And while we're on the topic of things to think about...I was wondering if you'd like to go to dinner with me. Not at Red Reef. Somewhere outside of town. Something nice."

"Are you saying Red Reef isn't nice?"

"You know what I mean," he said, smiling.

Instantly, she thought of kissing Brendan. But she also thought of how warm and welcoming the mere sight of Robbie had been when she'd first come to Port Bliss. And as she struggled with all of this, she realized she had something of an out.

"I leave for Richmond, Virginia, tomorrow morning, really early," she said. "Let me think about it during the trip."

"I can do that," he said. "I just thought it would be something nice to do for you after the ordeal you went through a few days ago."

"Oh, you heard about that?"

"I think the entire town has heard about it. Especially now that the woman who attacked you has been charged with the murder of Avery Decker."

"I'm just never going to stay out of the Port Bliss gossip circle, am I?"

"Doesn't seem like it."

Marie stepped back and closed the door on the hidden room. "Come on downstairs with me," she said. "Want some tea?"

"Sure."

They left the hidden room, and then the bedroom. As they made their way to the stairs, Marie stopped for a split second by Atticus Winslow's door, listening. It had become something of a habit, but she had yet to hear anything that clued her in to what he might be doing in there. It was yet another of the mysteries she found herself living with in a house that was slowly but surely starting to feel like her own.

***

Robbie called it a night shortly after his tea was gone. Marie appreciated this, as she had a very long drive ahead of her the following day. But before she settled in for the night, she leashed Boo and walked him outside, around the house, and toward the beach. They only walked several yards down the night-shrouded shore before she sat down and stared out to the ocean. Boo sat down beside her and stared as well.

"You have any general feeling about psychics, boy?" she asked.

His only response was turning his head to look at her for a moment before again watching the white caps rise and fall ahead of them.

Marie knew she would have to face the mystery of her mother when she returned from Richmond. There was no way she would ever be able to let it go. There were other mysteries beyond it, namely why June had a hidden room and how involved in the paranormal she had really been. But the current status of her mother had to come first.

She'd seen what likely were ghosts and then watched them disappear as Boo chased them. She had found a hidden room and been attacked by a killer. But the idea of tracking down the truth about her mother scared her more than any of that. It was a paralyzing realization, but one that she had to face. Somehow, it was easier to process it while she watched the ocean, forever coming in and going back out.

Marie sat there in the dark, Boo standing guard beside her, for another fifteen minutes or so. When she finally walked away from the beach, back to the ghostly grounds Great-Aunt June had left her, she felt like she was stepping across a threshold into a world where she was ready to find answers at any cost.

NOW AVAILABLE!

THE GHOSTLY GROUNDS:
MALICE AND LUNCH
(A Canine Casper Cozy Mystery—Book 3)

"The perfect romance or beach read, with a difference: its enthusiasm and beautiful descriptions offer an unexpected attention to the complexity of not just evolving love, but evolving psyches. It's a delightful recommendation for romance readers looking for a touch more complexity from their romance reads."
--Midwest Book Review (*For Now and Forever*)

THE GHOSTLY GROUNDS: MALICE AND LUNCH is Book #3 in a charming new cozy mystery series by bestselling author Sophie Love, author of *The Inn at Sunset Harbor* series, a #1 Bestseller with over 200 five-star reviews!

Marie Fortune, 39, a successful dog groomer in Boston, leaves the stressful life behind and heads to a small town in coastal Maine to create a new life. She remains intent on renovating the old, historic house her great-aunt left her and giving it a new life as a B&B. Yet there was one thing she couldn't plan for: the house is haunted. Two things, actually: her great-aunt also left her a dog—and he is far from a typical dog.

When Marie, her reputation for ghost-cleansing growing, is summoned to exorcise an old manor house, she finds more than she bargained for: an unexpected death occurs.

Worse, her trusted dog gets so sick, he is sent to the vet indefinitely.

Marie, on her own, must solve the murder and expel the ghosts all by herself.

Is she up to the task?

A page-turning cozy, packed with mystery, love, hauntings, travel, pets and food—anchored around a small town and a B&B in need of renovation that will capture your heart—THE GHOSTLY GROUNDS: MALICE AND LUNCH is an un-putdownable cozy that will keep you turning pages (and laughing out loud) late into the night.

"The romance is there, but not overdosed. Kudos to the author for this amazing start of a series that promises to be very entertaining."
--Books and Movies Reviews (*For Now and Forever*)

Sophie Love

#1 bestselling author Sophie Love is author of THE INN AT SUNSET HARBOR romantic comedy series, which includes eight books; of THE ROMANCE CHRONICLES romantic comedy series, which includes 5 books; and of the new CANINE CASPER cozy mystery series, which included three books (and counting).

Sophie would love to hear from you, so please visit www.sophieloveauthor.com to email her, to join the mailing list, to receive free ebooks, to hear the latest news, and to stay in touch!

BOOKS BY SOPHIE LOVE

THE CANINE CASPER COZY MYSTERY SERIES
THE GHOSTLY GROUNDS: MURDER AND BREAKFAST (Book #1)
THE GHOSTLY GROUNDS: DEATH AND BRUNCH (Book #2)
THE GHOSTLY GROUNDS: MALICE AND LUNCH (Book #3)
THE GHOSTLY GROUNDS: VENGEANCE AND DINNER (Book #4)

THE INN AT SUNSET HARBOR
FOR NOW AND FOREVER (Book #1)
FOREVER AND FOR ALWAYS (Book #2)
FOREVER, WITH YOU (Book #3)
IF ONLY FOREVER (Book #4)
FOREVER AND A DAY (Book #5)
FOREVER, PLUS ONE (Book #6)
FOR YOU, FOREVER (Book #7)
CHRISTMAS FOREVER (Book #8)

THE ROMANCE CHRONICLES
LOVE LIKE THIS (Book #1)
LOVE LIKE THAT (Book #2)
LOVE LIKE OURS (Book #3)
LOVE LIKE THEIRS (Book #4)
LOVE LIKE YOURS (Book #5)

Made in the USA
Coppell, TX
23 August 2021